After the Fall

After the Fall

A play by Arthur Miller

New York: The Viking Press

For my wife, Ingeborg Morath

After the Fall

Characters

QUENTIN

FELICE

HOLGA

DAN

FATHER

MOTHER

MAGGIE

ELSIE

LOU

LOUISE

MICKEY

CARRIE

LUCAS

CHAIRMAN

HARLEY BARNES

Nurses, porter, secretary, hospital attendant, a group of
boys, and passers-by

Act One

The action takes place in the mind, thought, and memory of Quentin.

> *Except for one chair there is no furniture in the conventional sense; there are no walls or substantial boundaries.*
>
> *The setting consists of three levels rising to the highest at the back, crossing in a curve from one side of the stage to the other. A stairway, center, connects them. Rising above all, and dominating the stage, is the blasted stone tower of a German concentration camp. Its wide lookout windows are like eyes which at the moment seem blind and dark; bent reinforcing rods stick out of it like broken tentacles.*
>
> *On the two lower levels are sculpted areas; indeed, the whole effect is neolithic, a lava-like, supple geography in which, like pits and hollows found in lava, the scenes take place. The mind has no color but its memories are brilliant against the grayness of its landscape. When people sit they do so on any of the abutments, ledges, or crevices. A scene may start in a confined area, but spread or burst out onto the entire stage, overrunning any other area.*
>
> *People appear and disappear instantaneously, as in the mind; but it is not necessary that they walk off the stage. The dialogue will make clear who is "alive" at any moment and who is in abeyance.*
>
> *The effect, therefore, will be the surging, flitting, instantaneousness of a mind questing over its own surfaces and into its depths.*
>
> *The stage is dark. Now there is a sense that some figure has moved in the farthest distance; a footstep is heard, then others. As light*

dimly rises the persons in the play move in a random way up from beneath the high back platform. Whispering emanates from them. Some sit at once, others come farther downstage, seem to recognize one another; still others move alone and in total separateness; in short, there is a totally random congeries of movements in a slow but not dreamlike rhythm. One of them, Quentin, a man in his forties, moves out of this mass and down the depth of the stage to the chair. This chair faces front, toward the audience. A sharp light now isolates it. All movement ceases. Quentin reaches forward over the chairback to shake the hand of the Listener, who, if he could be seen, would be sitting just beyond the edge of the stage itself.

QUENTIN: Hello! God, it's good to see you again! I'm very well. I hope it wasn't too inconvenient on such short notice. Fine, I just wanted to say hello, really. Thanks. *He sits on invitation.* How've you been? You look sunburned. . . . Oh! I've never been to South America, you enjoy it? That's nice. . . . Do I? I guess I am, I'm quite healthy—I do a lot of walking now. *Slight pause.* I started to call you a couple of times this year. Last year too. . . . Well, I lost the impulse; I wasn't sure what I wanted to say, and at my age it's discouraging to still have to go wandering around in one's mind. Actually, I called you on the spur of the moment this morning; I have a bit of a decision to make. You know—you mull around about something for months and all of a sudden there it is and you're at a loss for what to do. Were you able to give me two hours? It might not take that long, but I think it involves a great deal and I'd rather not rush. Fine.

He sets himself to begin, looks off.

Ah . . .

Interrupted, he turns back to Listener, surprised.

I've quit the firm, didn't I write you about that? Really! I was sure I'd written. . . . Oh, about fourteen months ago; a few weeks after Maggie died. . . . No, no. I've withdrawn completely. I still hold my interest, such as it is, but I'm out of it. . . . Well, it just got to where I couldn't concentrate on a case any more; not the way I used to. It's hard to describe; it all lost its necessity; I was going on because I'd started out to become a successful attorney, and I'd become one—I felt I was merely in the service of my own success. There has to be some semblance of a point, and I couldn't find it any more. Although I do wonder sometimes if I am simply trying to destroy myself. . . . Well, I have walked away from what passes for an important career. . . . Not very much, I'm afraid; I still live in the hotel, see a few people, read a good deal—*Smiles*—stare out the window. I don't know why I'm smiling; maybe I feel that's all over now, and I'll harness myself to something again. Although I've had that feeling before and done nothing about it, I—

Again, interrupted, he looks surprised.

God, I wrote you about *that*, didn't I? Maybe I dream these letters. . . . Mother died. Oh, it's four, five months ago, now. Yes, quite suddenly; I was in Germany at the time and . . . it's one of the things I wanted to talk to you about. I . . . met a woman there. *He grins.* I never thought it could happen again, but we became quite close. In fact, she's arriving tonight for some conference at Columbia. She's an archaeologist. . . . I'm not sure, you see, if I want to lose her, and yet it's outrageous to think of committing myself again. . . . Well, yes, but look at my life. A life, after all, is evidence, and I have two divorces in my safe-deposit box.

He stands, moves, thinks.

I tell you frankly I'm a little afraid. . . . Of who and what I'd be bringing to her. And I thought if I could say aloud what I see when I'm alone . . . Well, for example, this:

He sits again, leans forward.

You know . . . more and more I see that for many years I looked at life like a case at law. It was a series of proofs. When you're young you prove how brave you are, or smart; then, what a good lover; then, a good father; finally, how wise, or powerful or what-the-hell-ever. But underlying it all, I see now, there was a presumption. That one moved not in a dry circle but on an upward path toward some elevation, where . . . God knows what . . . I would be justified, or even condemned. A verdict, anyway. I think now that my disaster really began when I looked up one day . . . and the bench was empty. No judge in sight. And all that remained was the endless argument with oneself, this pointless litigation of existence before an empty bench. . . . Which, of course, is another way of

saying—despair, and no great news. Some of the best, most ener-
getic lawyers I know believe in nothing, and even find a joy in
proving again and again that men are worthless, including their
own clients. Despair can be a way of life, providing you believe in
it. And I say to myself, pick it up, take it to heart, and move on
again. Instead, I seem to be hung up, waiting for some . . . believ-
able sign. And the days and the months . . . and now the years . . .
are draining away. *Slight pause.* A couple of weeks ago I became
aware of a strange fact. With all this darkness, the truth is that every
morning when I awake, I'm full of hope! With everything I know
. . . I open up my eyes . . . I'm like a boy! For an instant there's
some . . . unformed promise in the air. I jump out of bed, I shave,
I can't wait to finish breakfast—and then . . . it seeps in my room,
the world, my life, and its pointlessness. And I thought . . . if I
could corner that hope, find what it consists of and either kill it for
a lie, or really make it mine . . .

Felice enters in sweater and skirt, sits on the floor.

FELICE: I just saw you walking by, that's all, and I thought, why
don't I talk to you? You do remember me, don't you?

QUENTIN, *with a glance at Felice*: For instance, I ran into a girl on
the street last month; I'd settled her divorce a few years ago and
she recognized me. And I hadn't had a woman in so long and she
obviously wanted to . . .

FELICE: No! I just wanted to be near you. I love your face. You
have a kind face. . . . You remember in your office, when my
husband was refusing to sign the papers?

QUENTIN, *to Listener*: It's this: somehow, whatever I look at, I
seem to see its death.

He turns to her.

FELICE: Well, see, he was always so childish alone with me; like a
little stubborn boy. And when you talked to him—I could see it,
he felt like a man. Like he had dignity. And me too. I felt like a
grown-up woman. And I swear . . . when we walked out of your
office, I . . . I almost loved him! And he asked me something when
we got down in the street. Should I tell you? Or do you know
already?

QUENTIN, *in frustration*: I'm afraid it's pointless, I don't know why I—

> *Breaks off, still to Listener.*

Well, just that he asked her to go to bed with him, one last time...

FELICE: How did you know that!

QUENTIN—*he is caught by her suddenly; his tone is answering her*: Because it's very hard to see the death of love, and simply walk away. *He is now turning to face her.*

FELICE: You think I should have?

QUENTIN: Well, what harm would it have done?

FELICE: That's what *I* wondered! Except, it would be funny, wouldn't it? The same day we got a divorce? See, I wanted it to mean something, the divorce!

QUENTIN: Honey... you never stop loving whoever you loved. Hatred doesn't wipe it out.

> *Louise appears, brushing her hair. Maggie sits up from the upper platform, her breathing beginning to be heard. And Quentin becomes active and agitated, and speaks to the Listener.*

Why do I make such stupid statements? I don't believe that! These goddamned women have injured me; have I learned nothing?

> *Holga appears beneath the tower, her arms full of flowers.*

HOLGA: Would you like to see Salzburg? I think they play *The Magic Flute* tonight.

> *Quentin is facing up to her. A pause. He turns back to Listener.*

QUENTIN: It's that... I don't know what I'd be bringing to that girl.

> *Holga is gone, and Maggie and Louise.*

I don't know what I believe about my own life! What? *He turns to Felice.* Well, death in the sense that she was trying so damned hard to be hopeful, and I...

FELICE: I don't deny he loved me, but... everything came down to how much mileage you got on a Volkswagen! I just wished we could get lost in some goddamn wilderness or something, and scream and bite each other and . . . and start going *toward* something!

QUENTIN: Well, you're in the wilderness now, aren't you? You live alone, leave the bed unmade, get a hamburger at three in the morning, sleep with who you like. You feel you're going toward something?

FELICE: I think so. I feel I'm good now, as a dancer . . . or almost. I almost feel free, when I dance. Not quite, but . . . sometimes I only have to think high and I go high; I have a long thought and I fly across the floor; sometimes, sometimes I'm almost exactly what I imagine, and when that happens . . .

> *She has danced out of sight.*

QUENTIN: Death in this sense: I'm sure her hope is real to her, but I sit there and see the day her legs will lose their spring, and her body will no longer follow those high leaping thoughts. . . . Yes, but there's always time to die, why reach for it? In fact, she came back again the other night, almost flew into my room! And it struck me with great force—how little I really believe in life.

> *Felice appears, standing, with a coat on; she is straight, nearly ecstatic.*

FELICE: I had my nose fixed! Are you very busy? The doctor took the bandage off but I put it back on. I wanted you to be the first. Do you mind?

QUENTIN: No. But why me?

FELICE: Because . . . remember that night when I came up here? I was trying to make up my mind . . . I mean there's something sort of insincere about changing your nose. I mean there could be. If that's all that makes or breaks you, the shape of a piece of cartilage? I mean if you're going to go through life building everything on *that* . . . You don't absolutely have to answer, but . . . I think you wanted to make love to me that night. Didn't you?

QUENTIN: I did, yes.

FELICE: I knew it! And it just clicked something for me. Because you really listened to me and didn't just try to roll me over. I felt it didn't matter what kind of nose I had, so I—I might as well have a short one! Can I show it to you?

QUENTIN: I'd like very much to see it.

FELICE: Close your eyes.

He does. She lifts the invisible bandage.

Okay.

He looks. She raises her arm in blessing.

I'll always bless you. Always!

He turns away, slowly returns to the chair as she walks into darkness.

QUENTIN, *to the Listener*: Maybe it's this; she meant nothing to me, it was a glancing blow, and yet it's not impossible that I stand in her mind like some corner she turned in her life. I feel like a mirror in which she somehow saw herself as . . . glorious. The truth is, I even liked her first nose better!

Two pallbearers in the distance carry an invisible coffin.

It's like my mother's funeral; I still hear her voice in the street sometimes, loud and real, calling my name. She's under the ground but she's not impressively dead to me. That whole cemetery . . . I saw it like a field of buried mirrors in which people saw themselves. I don't seem to know how to grieve. Or is it just some hardness in it bothers me?

Holga appears above, flowers in her arms.

God, maybe I ought to live alone; or maybe I don't believe that grief is grief unless it kills you.

Holga is gone. Dan appears. A nurse is whispering in his ear.

Like when I flew back and met my brother in the hospital.

The nurse hurries out, and Dan speaks to the empty air.

DAN: I'm so glad you got here, kid; I wouldn't have wired you but I don't know what to do. You have a good flight?

Now Father appears in a "bed." The same nurse is puffing up his pillow.

FATHER: Is that my sons in the hall? Where's my wife?

QUENTIN, *to Dan*: But what's the alternative? She's dead, he has to know.

FATHER: Why don't they come in? Where's my daughter?

DAN: But he was only operated on this morning. How can we walk in and say, "Your wife is dead"? It's like sawing off his arm. Suppose we tell him she's on her way, then give him a sedative?

QUENTIN: But Dan, I think it belongs to him, doesn't it? After fifty years you . . . owe one another a death?

DAN, *in agony*: Kid, the woman was his right hand. Without her he was never very much, you know. He'll fall apart.

QUENTIN: I can't agree; I think he can take it, he's got a lot of stuff.

> *Without halt, to the Listener:*

Which is hilarious! . . . Well, because! He was always the one who idolized the old man, and I saw through him from the beginning; suddenly we're changing places, like children in a game! I don't know what I am to anybody!

DAN, *as though he had come to a decision*: All right; let's go in, then.

QUENTIN: You want me to tell him?

DAN, *unwillingly, afraid but challenged*: I'll do it.

QUENTIN: I could do it, Dan.

DAN, *relieved*: All right; if you don't mind.

> *They turn together toward Father in the "bed." He does not see them yet. They move with the weight of their news.*

QUENTIN: It belongs to him, Dan, as much as his wedding.

> *He turns to the Listener as he walks.*

Or is it simply that . . .

> *They have come to a halt near Father's "bed."*

. . . I am crueler than he?

> *The nurse glances up at them and goes upstage, but waits there, apparently squinting into an upheld hypodermic needle. Now Father sees them and raises up his arm.*

FATHER: For cryin' out loud! Look who's here! I thought you were in Europe!

QUENTIN: Just got back. How are you?

DAN: You look wonderful, Dad.

FATHER: What do you mean, "look"? I *am* wonderful! I tell you, I'm ready to go through it again!

They laugh proudly with him.

I mean it—the way that doctor worries, I finally told him, "Look, if it makes you feel so bad you lay down and I'll operate!" Very fine man. I thought you'd be away couple months more.

QUENTIN, *hesitantly*: I decided to come back and—

DAN, *breaking in, his voice turning strange*: Sylvia'll be right in. She's downstairs buying you something.

FATHER: Oh, that's nice! I tell you something, fellas—that kid is more and more like Mother. Been here every day . . . Where is Mother? I been calling the house.

The slightest empty, empty pause.

DAN: One second, Dad, I just want to—

Crazily, without evident point, he starts calling, and moving up-stage toward the nurse. Quentin is staring at his father.

Nurse! Ah . . . could you call down to the gift shop and see if my sister . . .

FATHER: Dan! Tell her to get some ice. When Mother comes you'll all have a drink! I got a bottle of rye in the closet.

To Quentin, as Dan comes in closer:

I tell you, kid, I'm going to be young. I've been thinking all day since I woke up—Mother's right; just because I got old I don't have to act old. I mean we could go to Florida, we could—

QUENTIN: Dad.

FATHER: What? Is that a new suit?

QUENTIN: No, I've had it.

FATHER, *remembering—to Dan, of the nurse*: Oh, tell her glasses, we'll need more glasses.

Dan feels forced to turn and start out.

QUENTIN: Listen, Dad.

Dan halts, and turns back.

FATHER, *totally unaware*: Yeah?

QUENTIN—*he takes Father's hand*: Mother died.

> *Father's hand grips his abdomen as though he were stabbed; his right arm rises like a policeman ordering a stop. A gasp flies out of him.*

She had a heart attack last night on her way home.

FATHER: Oh, no, no, no, no.

QUENTIN, *grasping his hand again*: We didn't want to tell you but—

FATHER: Ahhh! Ahhh, no, no, no.

DAN: There's nothing anybody could have done, Dad.

FATHER—*he claps his hands together*: Oh! Oh! Oh!

QUENTIN, *grasping his hand again*: Now look, Dad, you're going to be all right, you'll—

FATHER—*it is all turning into a deep gasping for breath; he struggles on his "bed," half trying to get off, his head constantly turning as though he were looking for his wife*: Oh boy. Oh boy! No, no.

DAN: Now look, Dad, you're a hell of a fella. Dad, listen—

FATHER: God damn it! I couldn't take care of myself, I knew she was working too hard!

QUENTIN: Dad, it's not your fault, that can happen to anyone.

FATHER: But she was sitting right here. She was . . . she was right here!

> *Now he weeps uncontrollably into his hands. Quentin puts an awkward arm around him.*

QUENTIN: Pa . . . Pa . . .

> *Now Quentin grips him with both arms. Dan moves in close as though to share him. He lays a hand on Father's shoulder.*

FATHER: Oh, boys—she was my right hand!

> *He raises his fist and seems about to lose his control again.*

DAN: We'll take care of you, Dad. I don't want you to worry about—

FATHER: No-no. It's . . . I'll be all right. I'll . . . God! . . . Now I'm better! Now, *now* I'm better!

> *They are silent; he keeps shaking his head.*

So where is she?

QUENTIN: In the funeral parlor.

FATHER, *shaking his head—an explosive blow of air*: Paaaaaah!

QUENTIN: We didn't want to tell you but we figured you'd rather know.

FATHER: Ya. *Pats Quentin's hand.* Thanks. Thanks. I'll . . . *He looks up at Quentin.* I'll just have to be stronger.

QUENTIN: That's right, Dad.

FATHER, *to no one*: This . . . will make me stronger. *But the weeping threatens; he clenches his jaws, shakes his head, and indicates a point.* She was right here!

> *Lights go out on him and Dan. Quentin comes slowly to the Listener.*

QUENTIN: Yes, I'm proud I didn't kid him, it bothers me. I don't know, maybe that he took it so for granted I was also devastated. . . . This? I hadn't thought of this as grief. I hope it is.

> *The tower gradually begins to light.*

Still, a couple months later he bothered to register and vote. . . . Well, I mean . . . it didn't kill him either, with all his tears. I don't know what the hell I'm driving at! I—*He is caught by the bright tower.* I don't get the connection at the moment but . . . I visited a concentration camp in Germany. . . .

> *He has started toward the tower when Felice appears, raising her arm in blessing.*

FELICE: Close your eyes, okay?

QUENTIN, *turned by her force*: I don't understand why that girl sticks in my mind. . . . Yes!

> *He moves toward her now.*

She did; she offered me some . . . love, I guess. And if I don't return it . . . or if it doesn't change me somehow, it . . . it's like owing for a gift you didn't ask for.

FELICE: I'll always bless you!

> *Her arm raised, she walks into darkness.*

QUENTIN: When she left, I did a stupid thing. I don't understand it. There are two light fixtures on the wall of my hotel room. *Against his own disgust.* I noticed for the first time that they're . . . a curious distance apart. And I suddenly saw that if you stood between them—*He spreads out his arms*—you could reach out and rest your . . .

> *Just before he completely spreads his arms Maggie sits up; her breathing sounds. He drops his arms, aborting the image. Maggie goes dark.*

Maybe I can get to it later. I can't now. . . .

> *Now Holga appears and is bending to read the legend fixed to the wall of a torture chamber.*

Yes, with this woman . . . Holga. She took me there.

HOLGA, *turning to "him"*: It's a general description. No, I don't mind, I'll translate it.

> *She returns to the legend; he slowly approaches behind her.*

"In this camp a minimum of two hundred thousand Dutch, Belgian, Russian, Polish, French, and Danish prisoners of war were killed. Also, four thousand two hundred and seven refugees from the Spanish Republican Army. The door to the left leads into the chamber where their teeth were extracted for gold; the drain in the floor carried off the blood. At times instead of shooting, they were individually strangled to death. The barracks on the right were the bordello where women prisoners were forced to—"

QUENTIN, *touching her shoulder*: I think you've had enough, Holga.

HOLGA: No, if you want to see the rest . . . *She bursts into tears, but in silence, and quickly turns away.* Come, I don't mind.

QUENTIN, *taking her arm*: Let's walk, dear. Country looks lovely out there.

> *They walk. The light changes to day.*

Here, this grass looks dry; let's sit down.

> *They sit. Pause.*

I always thought the Danube was blue.

HOLGA: Only the waltz. Although it does change near Vienna. Out of some lingering respect for Strauss, I suppose.

QUENTIN: I don't know why this hit me so; I suddenly got a cracking headache in there.

HOLGA: I'm sorry. It's just that you seemed so interested in the Nazi period, and we were passing so close . . .

QUENTIN: No, I'm glad I saw it.

HOLGA, *starting to rise; she senses an estrangement*: I have some aspirin in the car.

QUENTIN, *lightly touching her*: We'll go soon. I just want to . . . sit for a minute.

HOLGA, *to raise his spirits*: You still want to see Salzburg?

QUENTIN: Oh, sure.

HOLGA: I'd love to show you Mozart's house. And the cafés are excellent there.

QUENTIN, *turning to her now*: Was there somebody you knew died here?

HOLGA: Oh, no. I feel people ought to see it, that's all. No one comes here any more. I've brought foreign colleagues once or twice.

QUENTIN: But why do you come back? It seems to tear you apart.

HOLGA: I suppose . . . one doesn't want to lose the past, even if it's dreadful. You're the first person I've met in a very long time who wants to talk about it.

QUENTIN: Yes, but I'm an American.

HOLGA: Oh, Americans too. In fact, when I first visited America after the war I was three days under questioning before they let me in. It was impossible to explain to them. How could one be in forced labor for two years if one were not a Communist? And of course, not being Jewish either, it was very suspicious. I was ready to turn back, I was so frightened. In fact, it was only when I told them I had blood relatives in several Nazi ministries that they were reassured. You see? Here it's not talked about, and outside it's not understood. It's as though fifteen years of one's life had simply vanished in some insane confusion. So I was very glad you were so interested.

QUENTIN, *glancing up at the tower*: I guess I thought I'd be indignant, or angry. But it's like swallowing a lump of earth. It's strange.

> *He starts to cover his eyes and she presses him to lie down, and speaks cheerfully . . .*

HOLGA: Come, lie down here for a while and perhaps—

QUENTIN: No, I'm—*He has fended off her hand.* I'm sorry, dear, I didn't mean to push you away.

HOLGA, *rebuffed and embarrassed*: I see wildflowers on that hill; I'll pick some for the car!

> *She gets up quickly.*

QUENTIN: Holga?

> *She continues off. He jumps up and hurries to her, turning her.*

Holga.

> *He does not know what to say.*

HOLGA, *holding back tears*: Perhaps we've been together too much. I could rent another car at Linz; perhaps we could meet in Vienna sometime.

QUENTIN: I don't want to lose you, Holga.

HOLGA: I understand that you're leaving soon. I never expected any . . .

QUENTIN: But you do expect something, everybody does. You're not a woman to go to bed just for the ride.

HOLGA: No, I'm not. But I have settled since several years to live for my work. I am not helpless alone. It's simply that from the moment you spoke to me I felt somehow familiar, and it was never so before. . . . It isn't a question of getting married; I am not ashamed this way. But I must have *something*.

QUENTIN: I don't give you anything? Tell me; because I've been told that before, but never so calmly.

HOLGA: You give me very much. . . . It's difficult for me to speak like this—I am not a woman who must be reassured every minute, those women are stupid to me.

QUENTIN: We're good friends, Holga; say it to me.

HOLGA: You have nothing; but perhaps that's all you want. I can understand that after what you've lived.

QUENTIN: That's not it, Holga; there's nothing as dull as adventure. I've had all I can use.

HOLGA: But perhaps that's all there is for you.

QUENTIN—*he turns her face to him*: Holga. Are you weeping . . . for *me*?

HOLGA: Yes.

QUENTIN, *struck*: Don't go away; not yet. Will you?

HOLGA: I hear your wings opening, Quentin.

QUENTIN: I don't want to abuse your feeling for me, you understand? The truth is—and I couldn't say this if I didn't trust you—I swear I don't know if I have lived in good faith. And the doubt ties my tongue when I think of promising anything again.

HOLGA: But how can one ever be sure of one's good faith?

QUENTIN, *surprised*: God, it's wonderful to hear you say that. All my women have been so goddamned sure!

HOLGA: But how can one ever be?

QUENTIN—*he kisses her gratefully*: Why do you keep coming back to this place?

Pause. Holga is disturbed, uncertain.

HOLGA: I . . . don't know. Perhaps . . . because I didn't die here.

QUENTIN—*turns quickly to Listener*: What?

HOLGA: Although that would make no sense! I don't really know!

QUENTIN—*goes to the chair*: That people . . . what? "Wish to die for the dead"? No, no, I can understand it; survival can be hard to bear. But I . . . I don't think I feel that way . . .

Maggie again appears in bed on the upper level; she begins to heave for breath. Her face is still indistinguishable. Instantly Quentin turns away as from an opposite side of the stage a piano is heard and a woman, Mother, is in midsong with a romantic ballad from a musical of the twenties.

Although I do think of my mother now, and she's dead. Yes!

He turns to Holga.

Maybe the dead do bother her.

HOLGA: It was the middle of the war. I had just come out of a class and there were leaflets on the sidewalk. A photograph of a concentration camp. And emaciated people. It was dropped there by British Intelligence; one tended to believe the British. I had had no idea. Truly. Any more, perhaps, than Americans know how a Negro lives. I was seventeen; I lived in my studies; I planned how to cut my hair differently. It is much more complicated than it seems later. There were many officers in my family. It was our country. It isn't easy to turn against your country; not in a war. There are always reasons—do Americans turn against America because of Hiroshima? No, there are reasons always.

Pause.

And I took the leaflet to my godfather—he was still commanding our Intelligence. And I asked if it were true. "Of course," he said, "why does it excite you?" And I said, "You are a swine. You are all swine." I threw my briefcase at him. And he opened it and put some papers in and asked me to deliver it to a certain address. And I became a courier for the officers who were planning to assassinate Hitler. . . . They were all hanged.

QUENTIN: Why not you?

HOLGA: They didn't betray me.

QUENTIN: Then why do you say good faith is never sure?

HOLGA, *after a pause*: It was my country . . . longer perhaps than it should have been. But I didn't know. And now I don't know how I could not have known. I can't imagine not knowing, now.

QUENTIN: Holga . . . I bless your uncertainty. Maybe that's why you're so wonderful to be with. You don't seem to be looking for some goddamned . . . moral *victory*. Forgive me, I didn't mean to be distant with you. I—*Looks up at the tower*—think this place frightens me! And how is that possible? All empty!

HOLGA: I'll get the flowers. And maybe we can buy some cheese and apples and eat while we drive!

She starts away.

QUENTIN: And you forgive me?

HOLGA—*turns, and with great love*: Yes! I'll be right back! And we'll go right away!

> *She hurries away.*

> *Quentin stands in stillness a moment; the presence of the tower bores in on him; its color changes; he now looks up at it and addresses the Listener.*

QUENTIN: But it's empty now! In fact, the view from here is rather pastoral; and the stone walls are warm in the sun, and quiet. I think . . . I may have imagined it more monstrous. Or bizarre. I helped a mason years ago before I went to college—I see the problem building such high walls in sandy soil . . . how dare one think of that? I think of the footings—they must go ten feet down. At least ten! I know footings! But I never thought the stones would look so ordinary.

> *Now he turns out.*

Why do I *know* something here? Even hollow now and empty, it has a face; and asks a sort of question: "What do you believe . . . as true as this?" Yes! Believers built this, maybe that's the fright—and I, without belief, stand here disarmed. I can see the convoys grinding up this hill; and I inside; no one knows my name and yet they'll smash my head on a concrete floor! And no appeal.

> *He turns quickly to the Listener.*

Yes! It's that I no longer see some last appeal, and here there was none either! Socialism once, then love; some final hope is gone that always saved before the end!

> *Mother appears; at the same time her coffin appears above.*

MOTHER: Not too much cake, darling, there'll be a lot of food at this wedding. *Calling upstage.* Fanny? Cut him a small piece . . . well, not *that* small!

QUENTIN: Mother! That's strange. And murder. Or is it her comfort brings her to me in this place?

MOTHER: Fanny? Not too hot ironing my husband's dress shirt! *Turns suddenly to an invisible boy.* You are going to wear garters tonight, Quentin, and don't argue with me. . . . Because it's my brother's wedding and your stockings are not to hang over your shoes!

QUENTIN—*he has started to laugh but it turns into*: Why can't I mourn her? And Holga wept in there . . . why can't I weep? Why do I feel an understanding with this slaughterhouse?

Now Felice appears, raising her arm.

I don't understand what I'm supposed to be to anyone!

Felice is gone. Mother laughs. He turns to her, addressing the Listener.

I don't know, some wedding in the family. I don't get it.

MOTHER—*her laughter turning bitter*: God! Why must every wedding in this family be a catastrophe! . . . Because the girl is pregnant, darling, and she's got no money, she's stupid, and I tell you this one is going to end up with a mustache! Five beautiful men like that and one after the other . . . I don't know where they *find* such women!

QUENTIN, *watching her, seated*: But what the hell has this to do with a concentration camp?

MOTHER: And wants a tight gown! As though she's fooling somebody! That's why, darling, when you grow up, I hope you learn how to disappoint people. Especially women. Never forget it dear, you're a man, and a man has all the choices. Will you stop playing with matches? *Slaps an invisible boy's hand.* You'll pee in bed! Why don't you practice your penmanship instead? You write like a monkey, darling.

QUENTIN, *shaking his head, glancing up at the tower*: I don't get it.

Father suddenly appears, holding an invisible phone to his ear. Quentin instantly stands.

MOTHER: And where is your father? If he went to sleep in a Turkish bath again, I'll . . .

Quentin is moving toward Father as though wanting to hear what he is saying in phone; he is making a shushing gesture to Mother.

What are you talking about, I didn't end up calling all the Turkish baths the night my brother Herbert got married? Forgot all about it . . . and nothing bothers him!

She laughs warmly. Quentin has arrived at Father, peers at his profile.

FATHER: Herman? Cable Hamburg.

MOTHER: Like the night of the Dempsey-Tunney fight.

QUENTIN: Ssh!

He turns back, eager to hear what Father is saying.

MOTHER: . . . The men's-room door gets stuck so by the time he gets out there's a new champion. Cost him a hundred dollars to go to the men's room!

FATHER: No, sixty thousand tons; sixty; Vera Cruz, the *Bismarck's* due.

MOTHER: But you mustn't laugh at him, he's a wonderful man, it's just that sometimes he can drive you out of your mind.

FATHER: Then cable Southampton, turn him back to Finland Monday. A.T.O.

MOTHER: My wedding? Oh, no dear, my wedding . . . there was happiness.

Quentin turns to her.

Well, look at your father; to this day he walks into a room you want to bow! Not like my sisters, one after the other running into the house, "Mama, I'm in love!" And with what? With who? I wasn't allowed to *see* your father till his father and Grandpa had agreed! . . . *Because*, I decided for once somebody was not going to break my mother's heart. . . . What are you talking about, of course I loved him! *Warmly*. He'd take me to a restaurant—one look at him and the waiters started moving tables around; if he saw a thick water glass he'd walk out; there could be a line around the block to a Broadway show, he'd go right up to the box office and they'd find two tickets. *Because*, dear—people know that this is a *man*. Even Doctor Strauss, at my wedding he came over to me says, "Rose, I can see it looking at him, you've got a wonderful man," and he was always in love with me, Strauss. . . . Oh, sure, but he was only a medical student then, didn't have a penny, my father wouldn't let him in the house. Who knew he'd end up so big in gallstones? That poor boy—used to bring me novels to read, poetry, philosophy, God knows what! One time we even sneaked off to hear Rachmaninoff together. . . .

She laughs sadly; with wonder more than bitterness:

That's why, you see, two weeks after we were married; sit down to dinner and Papa hands me a menu, and asks me to read it to him. . . . Couldn't *read*! I got so frightened I nearly ran away! . . . "Why"? Because your grandmother is such a fine, unselfish woman; two months in school and they put him into the shop! That's what some women are, my dear . . . and now he goes and buys her a new Packard every year and two more for his brothers! Damned fool, I could kill him! And what are we paying a chauffeur for, I can't find him half the time anyway! . . . Because if they're going to have chauffeurs I'm going to have a chauffeur—it's all our money anyway!

> *With a strange and deep fear:*

Please, darling, I want you to *draw* the letters, that scribbling is ugly, dear; and your posture, your speech, it can all be beautiful! Ask Miss Fisher, for years they kept my handwriting pinned up on the bulletin board; they made up a special new prize to give me on graduating day. God, I'll never forget it, valedictorian of the class with a scholarship to Hunter in my hand—*A blackness flows into her soul*—and I come home, and Grandpa says, "You're getting married!" It had never come into my mind! I was like . . . like with small wings, just getting ready to fly; I slept all year with the catalogue under my pillow. To learn, to learn everything! Oh, darling, the whole thing is such a mystery!

> *Father enters the area, talking to the young, invisible Quentin.*

FATHER: Quentin, would you get me the office on the phone? *To Mother as he kisses her lightly on the cheek:* Why would you call the Turkish bath?

MOTHER: I thought you forgot about the wedding.

FATHER: I wish I could but I'm paying for it.

MOTHER: He'll pay you back!

FATHER: I believe it, I just wouldn't want to hang by my hair that long.

> *He turns, goes to an invisible phone, stands.*

Herman? Hold the wire. *To Mother:* Why don't you both go up and get dressed?

MOTHER, *moving up the stairs*: I don't want to be late, now.

FATHER: There's time; she won't give birth if we're half hour late.

MOTHER: Don't be so smart! He fell in love, what's so terrible about that?

FATHER: They all fall in love on my money. Only I can't fall in love unless I pay for it. I married into a love nest! *He turns to the invisible Quentin, warmly smiling.* Did they pass a law that kid can't get a haircut? *Reaching into his pocket, tossing a coin.* Here, at least get a shine. *To Mother:* I'll be right up, dear, go ahead, get dressed. *In "phone":* Herman? The accountant still there? Put him on.

QUENTIN, *suddenly, recalling:* Oh, yes!

MOTHER: I'll put in your studs. God, he's so beautiful in a tuxedo!

> *She goes a distance out of the area but halts on the stair, turns, eavesdrops.*

FATHER: Billy? You finished? Well what's the story, where am I?

> *Quentin now turns up toward Mother on the stairs.*

QUENTIN: . . . Yes!

FATHER: Don't you read the papers? What'll I do with Irving Trust, I can't give it away. What bank?

> *Mother descends a step, alarmed.*

I been to every bank in New York, I can't get a bill paid, how the hell they going to lend me money? No-no, there's no money in London, there's no money in Hamburg, there's no money in Hamburg, there ain't a cargo moving in the world, the ocean's empty, Billy. . . . Now tell me the truth, where am I?

> *Pause. Mother descends another step. Quentin is below, watching her. Now Mother descends into the area. Father stands almost stiffly, as though to take a storm.*

MOTHER: What's that about? What are you "winding up"?

> *Father stands staring; he speaks unheard, but she seems to have heard an additional shocking fact, then another, and another.*

What are you talking about? When did this start? . . . Well, how much are you taking out of it? . . . You lost your mind? You've got over four hundred thousand dollars' worth of stocks, you can sell the . . . You sold those wonderful stocks! When? . . . Eight months! I just bought a new grand piano, why didn't you say something? And a silver service for my brother, and you don't say anything? . . .

> *More subdued, walks a few steps in thought.*

Well then, you'd better cash your insurance; you've got at least seventy-five thousand cash value. . . .

> *Halts, turning in shock.*

When?

> *Father is gradually losing his stance, his grandeur; he pulls his tie loose.*

All right, then—we'll get rid of my bonds. Do it tomorrow. . . . What do you mean? Well you get them back, I've got ninety-one thousand dollars in bonds you gave me. Those are my bonds. I've got bonds. . . .

> *Breaks off; open horror on her face and now a growing contempt.*

You mean you saw everything going down and you throw good money after bad? Are you some kind of a moron?

FATHER: You don't walk away from a business; I came to this country with a tag around my neck like a package in the bottom of the boat!

MOTHER: I should have run the day I met you!

FATHER, *as though stabbed*: Rose!

> *He sits, closing his eyes, his neck bent.*

MOTHER: I should have done what my sisters did, tell my parents to go to hell and thought of myself for once! I should have run for my life!

FATHER: Sssh, I hear the kids.

> *A sharp shaft of light opens a few yards away and he glances toward it.*

MOTHER: I ought to get a divorce!

FATHER: Rose, the college men are jumping out of windows!

MOTHER: But your last dollar? *Bending over, into his face*: You are an idiot!

> *Her nearness forces him to stand; they look at each other, strangers.*

QUENTIN—*he looks up at the tower*: Yes! For no reason—they don't even ask your name!

FATHER—*he looks toward the column of light*: Somebody crying? Quentin's in there. You better talk to him.

> *Quentin walks upstage, away from the light. She goes in some trepidation toward it. A foot or so from it she halts.*

MOTHER: Darling? You better get dressed. Don't cry, dear, it'll be all right. He'll come back bigger than ever!

> *She is stopped short by something "Quentin" has said.*

What *I* said? Why, what did I say? . . . Are you crazy? I'd never say a thing like that, I thought you were upstairs. Well I was a little angry, that's all, but I never said *that*. I think he's a wonderful man! *Laughs*. How could I say a thing like that? Quentin!

> *The light rapidly fades, and as though he is disappearing she extends her arms toward the fading light.*

But I didn't say anything!

> *With a cry toward someone lost.*

Darling, I didn't say anything!

> *Instantly Holga appears beneath the tower, with flowers in her arms. She looks about for him.*

HOLGA: Quentin? Quentin?

> *He is still staring at Mother, from whom he turns toward Holga. Now Holga sees him and comes down to him.*

Look! The car will be all sweet inside!

QUENTIN—*he absently sniffs the flowers, staring at her*: You love me, don't you?

HOLGA: Yes.

QUENTIN, *glancing up at the tower*: Do you ever feel when you come here some vague . . . complicity?

HOLGA: Quentin . . . no one they didn't kill can be innocent again.

QUENTIN—*slight pause*: Then how do you get so purposeful, Holga? You work so hard, you seem so full of joy and hope.

HOLGA: While I was getting the flowers just now I thought I ought to tell you something. In a bombing once I lost my memory, and wandered everywhere with crowds across the countryside looking for a safe place. Every day, one turned away from people dying on the roads. Until one night I tried to jump from the railing of a bridge. An old soldier pulled me back and slapped my face and made me follow him; he'd lost a leg at Stalingrad, was furious that I would kill myself; I walked behind his crutches over Germany looking for some sign of who I'd been. And suddenly there was a door with a tremendous lion's-head brass knocker; I ran; I knocked; my mother opened it. My life came back! And I turned to ask the soldier in; to thank him; to feed him; to give him everything I had! But he was gone. I've been told that I imagined him, but even now at times I turn a corner and expect to find him. If we could even . . . nod to one another! I know how terrible it is to owe what one can never pay. And for a long time after I had the same dream each night—that I had a child; and even in the dream I saw that the child was my life; and it was an idiot. And I wept, and a hundred times I ran away, but each time I came back it had the same dreadful face. Until I thought, if I could kiss it, whatever in it was my own, perhaps I could rest. And I bent to its broken face, and it was horrible . . . but I kissed it.

QUENTIN: Does it still come back?

HOLGA: At times. But it somehow has the virtue now . . . of being mine. I think one must finally take one's life in one's arms, Quentin.

She takes his hand.

Come, I think they play *The Magic Flute* tomorrow. You like *The Magic Flute*?

QUENTIN—*he kisses her*: One thing about you, you tell the goddamned funniest stories!

HOLGA—*hits him and mock-pouts*: You're making fun of me!

QUENTIN: Let's get out of this dump, and . . . where we going?

HOLGA, *laughing*: Salzburg!

QUENTIN: I'll race you to the car, last one there's a rotten egg. Or do you say a rancid wurst?

HOLGA, *laughing*: Okay, I'm racing!

> *She gets set.*

QUENTIN: Go!

> *They start running, but while she goes off into darkness Quentin comes down to the chair.*

QUENTIN: I miss her badly. And yet, I can't sign my letters to her "With love." I put "Sincerely" or "As ever," some such brilliant evasion. I've lost the sense of some absolute necessity, I think. Living alone does that; I walk down the street, I see the millions of apartment windows lighting up—I swear I don't understand how each man knows which door to go to. Can they all be in love? Is that what sorts them out? I don't think so; it's some kind of innocence, a deep belief that all their destinations are ordained. With me, whether I open a book or think of marrying again, it's so damned clear I've chosen what I do—it cuts the strings between my hands and heaven. It sounds foolish, but I feel . . . unblessed. And I look back at when there seemed to be a kind of plan, some duty in the sky. I had a dinner table, and a wife, a child, and the world so wonderfully threatened by injustices I was born to correct! How fine! Remember? When there were good people and bad people? And how easy it was to tell! The worst son of a bitch, if he loved Jews and Negroes and hated Hitler—he was a buddy. Like some kind of paradise compared to this. . . . Until I begin to look at it.

> *Elsie appears, a beach robe hanging from her shoulders, her arms out of the sleeves, her back to us; she is fixing her wet hair in an invisible mirror.*

God, when I think of what I believed, I want to hide!

> *He stands, moves toward her.*

. . . Yes, but I wasn't all that young! You would think a man of thirty-two would know that when a guest, changing out of a wet bathing suit in his bedroom . . .

> *Elsie, as he approaches, turns to him, and her robe slips off one shoulder.*

and just stands there with her two bare faces hanging out . . .

ELSIE: Oh, are you through working? Why don't you swim now? The water's just right.

QUENTIN, *with a laugh of great pain, crying out*: I tell you I believed she didn't know she was naked! It's Eden!... Well, she was *married*! How could a woman who can tell when the Budapest String Quartet is playing off key, who refuses to wear silk stockings because the Japanese have invaded Manchuria, whose husband—my friend, a saintly professor of law—is editing my first appeal to the Supreme Court on the grass outside that window— I could see the top of his head past her tit, for God's sake!... Of course I understood, but it's what you allow yourself to admit! To admit what you see endangers principles!

> *Elsie leaves the "room" and crosses to where Louise sits. Quentin turns to them. They are talking in an intense whisper. He now approaches them from behind, halts, turns to the Listener.*

You know? When two women are whispering, and they stop abruptly when you appear . . .

ELSIE and LOUISE, *turning to him after an abrupt stop to their talking*: Hi.

> *In the background Lou appears, reading a brief—a tender, kindly man, in shorts.*

QUENTIN: . . . The subject must have been sex. And if one of them is your wife . . . she must have been talking about you.

ELSIE, *as though to get him to go*: Lou's behind the house, reading your brief. He says it's superb!

QUENTIN: I hope so. I've been kind of nervous about what he'd say.

ELSIE: I wish you'd tell him that, Quentin! Will you? Just how much his opinion means to you. It's important you tell him.

QUENTIN: I'll be glad to. *Awkwardly glancing from Louise back to her*: Nice here, isn't it?

ELSIE: It's enchanting. *Taking in Louise*: I envy you both so much!

QUENTIN: See you. Glad you could come.

ELSIE—*gets up, goes past Lou*: I want one more walk before the train, dear. Did you comb your hair today?

LOU, *closing the brief*: I think so. Quentin! This is superb! It's hardly like a brief at all; there's a majestic quality, like a classic

ELSIE—*a sudden flash of contempt; to Lou*: This is hardly the time for illusions!

With a smash of light Mother appears, and Father slumped in a chair beside her.

MOTHER: You *idiot*!

Quentin is shocked, turns quickly to Mother.

My *bonds*?

She and Father are gone. Instantly, as before, Holga appears under the tower, flowers in her hand, looking about for him.

HOLGA: Quentin?

He quickly turns his head toward her. She is gone.

QUENTIN, *alone*: How do you believe again?

Felice appears.

FELICE: I'll always bless you!

She turns and walks into the dark. The wall appears with the two light fixtures.

QUENTIN: The other night, when that girl left . . . I . . .

Turns to the wall. The fixtures light up. But he turns away, agonized.

I'll try to get to it . . .

ELSIE: Come, dear, you haven't even swum. Let's enjoy this weekend!

She walks off with Lou, kissing his cheek.

QUENTIN, *watching them go*: Then why does something seem to fall apart? Was it ever whole?

Louise now stands up from the beach chair. She turns, addresses an empty space.

LOUISE: Quentin?

QUENTIN—*he turns his eyes to the ground, then speaks to the Listener*: Wasn't that a terrifying thing, what Holga said?

LOUISE: I've decided to go into psychoanalysis.

QUENTIN, *still to Listener*: To take up your life, like an idiot child?

LOUISE: I want to talk about some things with you.

QUENTIN: But can anybody really do that?

He turns toward Louise now guiltily.

Kiss his life?

LOUISE, *as though he had not answered—speaking toward the empty space*: Quentin?

He is drawn to the spot she is concentrating her gaze on. Tension rises in him as he arrives in her line of sight and faces her.

You don't have to pick up Betty now, she enjoys playing there. *Steeling her shy self.* I've got to make a decision.

QUENTIN: About what?

LOUISE, *in fear*: About everything.

QUENTIN: What do you mean?

LOUISE—*at a loss for an instant*: Sit down, will you?

She sits, gathering her thoughts. He hesitates, as though pained at the memory, and also because at the time he lived this it was an agony. And as he approaches his chair he speaks to the Listener.

QUENTIN: It was like . . . a meeting. In seven years we had never had a meeting. Never, never what you'd call . . . a meeting.

LOUISE: We don't seem . . .

A long pause while she peers at a forming thought—

married.

QUENTIN: We?

LOUISE—*it is sincere, what she says, but she has had to learn the words, so there is the faintest air of a formula in her way of speaking*: You don't pay any attention to me.

QUENTIN, *puzzled*: When?

LOUISE: You never did. But I never realized it till . . . recently.

QUENTIN, *to help her*: You mean like Friday night? When I didn't open the car door for you?

LOUISE: Well, that's a small thing, but it's part of what I mean, yes.

QUENTIN: But I told you; you always opened the car door for yourself.

LOUISE: I've always done everything for myself, but that doesn't mean it's right. Everybody notices it, Quentin.

QUENTIN: What?

LOUISE: The way you behave toward me. I don't . . . *exist*. People are supposed to find out about each other. I am not all this uninteresting, Quentin. Many people, men *and* women, think I *am* interesting.

QUENTIN: Well, I—*Breaks off*. I—*Breaks off*. I . . . don't know what you mean.

LOUISE: I know you don't. You have no conception of what a woman is. You think I'm some sort of . . . I don't know what I am to you.

QUENTIN: But I do pay attention—just last night I read you my whole brief.

LOUISE: Quentin, you think reading a brief to a woman is talking to her?

QUENTIN: But that's what's on my mind.

LOUISE: But if that's all on your mind what do you need a wife for?

QUENTIN: Now what kind of a question is that?

LOUISE: Quentin, that's the question!

QUENTIN—*slight pause; with fear, astonishment*: What's the question?

LOUISE: What am I to you? Do you . . . do you ever *ask* me anything? Anything personal?

QUENTIN, *with rising alarm*: But Louise, what am I supposed to ask you? I *know* you!

LOUISE: No.

She stands with dangerous dignity.

You don't know me.

Pause. She proceeds now with caution.

I don't intend to be ashamed of myself any more, I used to think it was normal; or even that you don't see me because I'm not worth seeing. But I think now that you don't really see any woman. Except in some ways your mother. You do sense her feelings; you do know when she's unhappy or anxious, but not me. Or any other woman.

Elsie appears, about to drop her robe.

QUENTIN: That's not true, though. I . . .

LOUISE: Elsie's noticed it too.

QUENTIN, *guiltily snapping away from the vision of Elsie*: What?

LOUISE: She's amazed at you.

QUENTIN: Why, what'd she say?

LOUISE: You don't seem to . . . register the fact that a woman is *present.*

QUENTIN: Oh. *He is disarmed, confused, and silent.*

LOUISE: And you know how she admires you.

Quentin nods seriously. Suddenly he turns out the Listener and bursts into an agonized, ironical laughter. He abruptly breaks it off, and returns to silence before Louise.

Louise speaks with uncertainty; it is her first attempt at confrontation.

Quentin?

He stands in silence.

Quentin?

He is silent.

Silence is not going to solve it any more. I can't live this way. Quentin?

QUENTIN—*pause; he gathers courage*: Maybe I don't speak because the one time I did tell you my feelings you didn't get over it for six months.

LOUISE, *angered*: It wasn't six months, it was a few weeks. I did over-react, but it's understandable. You come back from a trip and tell me you'd met a woman you wanted to sleep with?

QUENTIN: That's not the way I said it.

LOUISE: It's exactly the way. And we were married a year.

QUENTIN: It is not the way I said it, Louise. It was an idiotic thing to tell you but I still say I meant it as a compliment; that I did not touch her because I realized what you meant to me. And for damn near a year you looked at me as though I were some kind of a monster who could never be trusted again.

LOUISE: Well that's in *your* mind. I've completely forgotten it.

QUENTIN: Is it only in my mind if you can still distort it this way?

LOUISE: Quentin, I am not your mother or some third party to whom you can come running with reports of your conquests!

QUENTIN: You see? This is what I mean! What conquests? How can I talk if you are going to blow everything up into a—a—

LOUISE: Quentin, I didn't bring her up, you did.

QUENTIN: Because I know you have never forgiven it, and I can't talk if I have to watch every word I say.

LOUISE, *astonished*: You mean you have to watch every word you say?

QUENTIN: Well, not every word, but—but—

LOUISE, *looking at him with new eyes*: Well, I had no idea!

QUENTIN, *pleading*: Now, look, Louise . . . I didn't mean it exactly that way!

LOUISE, *horrified*: I had no idea you were . . . dishonest with me.

QUENTIN, *drowning in guilt*: Well what did I say? What are you looking at me like that for?

> *With her hands thrust into her hair she rushes away, a stifled cry in her throat. He calls after her.*

Louise!

> *Immediately to the Listener:*

And why do I believe she's right? . . . That's the point! . . . Yes, now, now! It's innocence, isn't it? The innocent are always better, aren't they? Then why can't I be innocent?

> *Elsie appears, about to drop her robe.*

Why couldn't I simply say, "Louise, your best friend is treacherous;

your new-found dignity suits her purpose"? . . . No, no, it isn't only that Elsie tempted me, it's worse. If I see a sin why is it in some part mine?

Elsie vanishes as the tower appears.

Even this slaughterhouse! Could I kill Jews? Throw ice water on prisoners of war and let them freeze to death? Why does something in this place touch my shoulder like an accomplice? . . . Huh? Please, yes, if you think you know.

Mother appears. He turns to her.

In what sense treacherous?

MOTHER: What poetry he brought me! He understood me, Strauss. And two weeks after the wedding, Papa hands me the menu. To *read*!

QUENTIN: Huh! Yes! And to a little boy . . . who knows how to read; a powerful reader, that little boy!

MOTHER: I want your handwriting beautiful, darling; I want you to be . . .

QUENTIN: . . . an accomplice!

MOTHER, *turning on Father, who sits dejectedly*: My *bonds*? And you don't even tell me anything? Are you a moron?

QUENTIN—*he watches her go dark, and speaks to the Listener. The tower remains alive*: Yes, yes, I understand, but . . . Why is the world so treacherous? Shall we lay it all to mothers? You understand? The sickness is much larger than my skull; aren't there mothers who keep dissatisfaction hidden to the grave, and do not split the faith of sons until they go in guilt for what they did not do? And I'll go further—here's the final bafflement for me—is it altogether good to be not guilty for what another does?

Mickey appears coming to Quentin, who turns to him.

MICKEY: The brief is fine, kid; I swear it almost began to move me. *To Louise, grinning*: You proud of him?

LOUISE—*she starts off*: Yes! Lou and Elsie are here.

MICKEY: Oh! I didn't know. You look wonderful, Louise, look all excited!

LOUISE: Thanks! It's nice to hear.

She shyly, soundlessly laughs, glancing at Quentin, and goes.

MICKEY—*pause; his smile transforms instantly to a shy grin*: You got trouble?

QUENTIN, *embarrassed*: I don't think so. She's going into psycho-analysis.

The tower dies out.

MICKEY: You got trouble, then. *Laughs.* But she'll be more interesting. Although for a while she'll probably be talking about her rights.

QUENTIN: Really? That's just what she was talking about!

MICKEY—*shakes his head, laughing joyfully*: I love women! I think maybe you got married too young; I did too. Although, *you* don't fool around, do you?

QUENTIN: I don't, no.

MICKEY: Then what the hell are you so guilty about?

QUENTIN: I am?

MICKEY: She loves you, Quent.

QUENTIN: I guess so, ya.

MICKEY: Maybe you ought to— See, when it first happened to me, I set aside five minutes a day just imagining my wife as a stranger. As though I hadn't made her yet. You got to generate some respect for her mystery. Start with five minutes; I can go as long as an hour, now.

QUENTIN: Makes it seem like a game though, doesn't it?

MICKEY: Well it is, isn't it, in a way? As soon as there's two people you can't be absolutely sincere, can you? I mean she's not your rib.

QUENTIN: I guess that's right, yes.

Pause.

MICKEY: Where's Lou?

QUENTIN, *pointing*: They're down swimming. You want to swim?

MICKEY: No.

He walks to a point, looks down as over a cliff.

That dear man; look at him, he never learned how to swim, always paddled like a dog. I used to love that man. I still do.

He sits on his heels, draws in the earth.

I'm sorry you didn't get into town two weeks ago when I called you.

QUENTIN: Why, is there some . . . ?

MICKEY: Well, I called you, Quent, I called you three times wanting to talk to you.

He gets up, stands, hands in pockets, glancing at the ground.

I've been subpoenaed.

QUENTIN, *shocked*: Oh, God! The Committee?

MICKEY: Yes. I wish you'd have come into town. . . . But it doesn't matter now.

QUENTIN: I had a feeling it was something like that. I guess I . . . didn't want to know any more. I'm sorry, Mick.

To Listener:

Yes, not to see, not to see!

A long pause. They find it hard to look directly at each other. Mickey picks up a stick, gouges at it with his thumbnail.

MICKEY: I've been going through hell, Quent. It's a strange thing —to have to examine what you stand for; not theoretically, but on a life-and-death basis. A lot of things don't stand up.

QUENTIN: I guess the main thing is not to be afraid.

MICKEY: Yes. *Pause.* I don't think I am, any more. I was, two weeks ago; I shook when the marshal came into the office and handed me that pink piece of paper. I really shook. It was dreadful. My knees shook.

A pause. Both sit staring ahead. Finally, Mickey turns and looks at Quentin, who now faces him. Mickey tries to smile.

You may not be my friend any more.

QUENTIN—*tries to laugh it away, a terror rising in him*: Why?

MICKEY: I'm going to tell the truth.

Pause.

QUENTIN: How do you mean?

MICKEY: I'm . . . going to name names.

QUENTIN, *incredulously*: Why?

MICKEY: Because . . . I want to. I don't want this concealment any more. Fifteen years, wherever I go, whatever I talk about, the feeling is always there that I'm deceiving people. Like living in an occupied country, half in the dark.

QUENTIN: But you only belonged for a few months, didn't you?

MICKEY: Yes, but it was a commitment, Quent. I'm sorry we never got to talk about it; I've never really gone along with this Fifth Amendment silence, I think it's insincere; a man ought to take the rap for what he's been.

QUENTIN: But why couldn't you just tell about yourself?

MICKEY: I have. They're playing for keeps, kid; they want the names, and they mean to destroy anyone who—

QUENTIN: I think it's a mistake, Mick. All this is going to pass, and I think you'll regret it. And anyway, how can they destroy you?

MICKEY—*slight pause*: Quent, I'll be voted out of the firm if I don't testify.

QUENTIN: Oh, no! Max has always talked against this kind of thing!

MICKEY: I've had it out with Max.

QUENTIN: I can't believe it! What about DeVries?

MICKEY: DeVries was there, and Burton, and most of the others. I wish you'd have seen their faces when I told them. Men I've worked with for thirteen years. Played tennis; intimate friends, you know? And as soon as I said I had been—stones.

> *The tower lights.*

QUENTIN, *to the Listener*: Everything is one thing! You see? I don't know what we are to one another! Or rather, rather what we ought to be!

MICKEY: Quent, I could feel their backs turning on me. It was horrible! As though—they would let me die.

> *Maggie appears in her bed, and her breathing is heard.*

MAGGIE: Quentin?

> *Quentin barely glances at her and turns away, pacing up and down before the Listener. As Mickey resumes, Maggie and her deep-drawn breathing fade away.*

MICKEY: I only know one thing, Quent, I want to live an open life, a straightforward, open life!

> *Lou enters in bathing trunks, instantly overjoyed at seeing Mickey.*

LOU: Mick! I *thought* I heard your voice! *Grabs his hand.* How are you?

> *Holga appears beneath the tower with flowers, and in a moment disappears.*

QUENTIN: How do you dare make promises again? I have lived through all the promises, you see?

MICKEY: Pretty good, Lou. I intended to call you tomorrow.

LOU: Really? I was going to call *you*; about a little problem I— *Uncertain*: May I?

MICKEY: Of course, Lou! You can always call me. I've got guests at home. *Grasps Lou's arm.* Give my best to Elsie.

LOU, *relieved*: I'll ring you tomorrow! And thank you, Mickey!

> *The gratitude seems to stab Mickey, who is already a few yards away, and he turns back,* resolves *to turn back.*

MICKEY: What . . . was the problem, Lou?

LOU, *relieved, hurrying to him like a puppy*: Just the question of publishing my book now. Elsie's afraid it will wake up all the sleeping dogs again. . . .

MICKEY—*pause*: But don't you have to take that chance? I think a man's got to take the rap, Lou, for what he's done, for what he is. I think what you hide poisons you. After all, it's your work.

LOU: I feel exactly that way! *Grabs his arm.* Golly, Mick! Why don't we get together as we used to? I miss all that wonderful talk! Of course I know how busy you are now, but—

MICKEY: Lou.

> *Pause.*

LOU: Yes, Mick. I'll meet you anywhere you say!

MICKEY: Elsie coming up?

LOU: You want to see her? I could call down to the beach.

>   *He starts off; Mickey stops him.*

MICKEY: Lou.

LOU, *sensing something odd*: Yes, Mick.

QUENTIN, *facing the sky*: Dear God.

MICKEY: I've been subpoenaed.

LOU: No!

>   *Mickey nods, looks at the ground. Lou grips his arm.*

Oh, I'm terribly sorry, Mick. I was afraid of that when they called me. But can I say something—it might ease your mind: once you're in front of them it all gets remarkably simple!

QUENTIN: Oh, dear God!

LOU: Really, it's not as terrible as it seems to you now; everything kind of falls away excepting one's . . . one's self. One's truth.

MICKEY—*slight pause*: I've already been in front of them, Lou. Two weeks ago.

LOU: Oh! Then what do they want with you again?

MICKEY—*pause. A fixed smile on his face*: I asked to be heard again.

LOU, *puzzled, open-eyed*: Why?

MICKEY— *he carefully forms his thought*: Because I want to tell the truth.

LOU, *with the first rising of incredulous fear*: In . . . what sense? What do you mean?

MICKEY: Lou, when I left the hearing room I didn't feel I had spoken. Something else had spoken, something automatic and inhuman. I asked myself, what am I protecting by refusing to answer? Lou, you must let me finish! You must. The Party? But I despise the Party, and have for many years. Just like you. Yet there is something, something that closes my throat when I think of telling names. What am I defending? It's a dream, now, a dream of solidarity, but hasn't that died a long time ago? The fact is, I have no solidarity with the people I could name—excepting for you. And not because we were Communists together, but because we were young together. Because we—when we talked it was like—monks probably talk, like some brotherhood opposed to all the world's injustice. It's you made my throat close, just the love whenever we saw one another. But what created that love, Lou? Wasn't it a respect for truth, a hatred of hypocrisy? Therefore, in the name of that love, I ought to be true to myself now. It would be easier, in a sense, to do what you did and stick with it; I would keep your friendship, but lose myself. Because the truth, Lou, my truth, is that I think the Party *is* a conspiracy. . . . Let me finish. I think we *were* swindled; they took our lust for the right and used it for Russian purposes. And I don't think we can go on turning our backs on the truth simply because reactionaries are saying it. What I propose—is that we try to separate our love for one another from this political morass. It was not the Party we loved, it was each other's truth. And I've said nothing just now that we haven't told each other for the past five years.

LOU: Then . . . what's your proposal?

MICKEY: That we go back together. Come with me. And answer the questions. I was going to tell you this tomorrow.

LOU: Name . . . the names?

MICKEY: Yes. I've talked to all the others in the unit. They've agreed, excepting for Ward and Harry. They cursed me out, but I expected that.

LOU, *dazed*: Let me understand—you are asking my permission to name me? *Pause.* You may not mention my name. *He begins physically shaking.* And if you do it, Mickey, you are selling me for your own prosperity. If you use my name I will be dismissed. You will ruin me. You will destroy my career.

MICKEY: Lou, I think I have a right to know exactly why you—

LOU: Because if everyone broke faith there would be no civilization! That is why that Committee is the face of the Philistine! And it astounds me that you can speak of truth and justice in relation to that gang of cheap publicity hounds! Not one syllable will they get from me! Not one word from my lips! No—your elevenroom apartment, your automobile, your money are not worth this.

He strides toward the edge of the area.

MICKEY, *stiffened*: That's a lie! You can't reduce it all to money, Lou! *That is false!*

LOU, *turning on him*: There is only one truth here. You are terrified! They have bought your soul!

He starts out again.

MICKEY, *angrily, but contained*: And yours? Lou! Is it all yours, your soul?

LOU, *beginning to show tears*: How dare you speak of my—?

MICKEY, *quaking with anger*: You've got to take it if you're going to dish it out, don't you? Have you really earned this high moral tone—this . . .

Elsie appears in the farthest distance, slowly coming toward them as though from a beach, her robe open, her head raised up toward the breeze, toward longing, toward the sky.

perfect integrity? I happen to remember when you came back from your trip to Russia; and I remember who made you throw your first version into my fireplace!

LOU, *almost screaming—after a glance toward Elsie*: The idea!

MICKEY: I saw you burn a true book and write another that told lies! Because she demanded it, because she terrified you, because she has taken your soul!

LOU, *shaking his fist in the air*: I condemn you!

MICKEY: But from your conscience or from hers? Who is speaking to me, Lou?

LOU: You are a monster!

He bursts into tears, walks off toward Elsie; he meets her in the near distance, says a few words, and her face shows horror. At the front of stage Mickey turns and looks across the full width toward Quentin at the farthest edge of light, and, reading Quentin's feelings:

MICKEY: I guess you'll want to get somebody else to go over your brief with you.

Quentin, indecisive, but not contradicting him, now turns to him.

Good-by, Quentin.

QUENTIN, *in a dead tone*: Good-by, Mickey.

Mickey goes out as Elsie and Lou rush down, she in a near-hysteria. As they arrive, Louise appears, stands watching.

ELSIE: Did you hear? *Including Louise in her glance.* Did you hear? He's a *moral idiot*!

Quentin turns to her; something perhaps in his gaze or in the recesses of her mind makes her close her robe, which she holds tightly shut. And to Quentin . . .

Isn't that *incredible*?

QUENTIN, *quietly*: Yes.

ELSIE: After such friendship! Such love between them! And for so many years!

The camp tower comes alive, and Quentin moves out of this group, slowly toward it, looking up.

LOU, *stunned*: And only this spring, brought me an expensive briefcase for my birthday!

ELSIE: And named his son Louis after you! Who can understand this?

Above, Holga appears as before, carrying flowers. She is a distance away from Quentin, who turns to her.

QUENTIN: You love me, don't you?

HOLGA: Yes.

An instant's hesitation and he turns quickly to Listener, and cries out.

QUENTIN: Is it that I'm looking for some simple-minded constancy that never is and never was?

He turns to Elsie, who is lifting Lou to his feet and kisses him.

How tenderly she lifts him up—now that he is ruined.

Elsie walks off with Lou, her arm around him, and kissing his cheek. Quentin watches them go.

Still, that could be a true kiss. Or is there no treason but only man, unblamable as trees or cats or clouds? . . . Yes, I do, I see it; but if that is what we are, what will keep us safe?

> *Louise appears.*

Or is the question foolish?

LOUISE: I had a dream. I want to tell you about it.

QUENTIN, *in pain*: Are we ever safe?

LOUISE: I was standing beside a high mountain. With my legs cut off.

> *He picks up a brief, looks into it.*

Must you work tonight?

QUENTIN: It's Lou's case. I have a pile of stuff. *Slight pause.* Well, I can do it later. What is it?

LOUISE: Never mind.

QUENTIN—*he sits at once, as though remembering some resolution to act well*: I'm sorry, Louise. What'd you want to say?

LOUISE: I'm trying to understand why you got so angry with me at the party the other night.

QUENTIN: I wasn't *angry*; I simply felt that every time I began to talk you cut in to explain what I was about to say.

LOUISE: Well, I'd had a drink; I was a little high. I felt happy, I guess, that you weren't running for cover when everybody else was.

QUENTIN: Yes, but Max was there, and DeVries, and they don't feel they're running for cover. I only want to win Lou's case, not some moral victory over the firm. I felt you were putting me out on a limb.

LOUISE: Quentin, I saw you getting angry when I was talking about that new anti-virus vaccine.

> *He tries to remember, believing she is right.*

What is it? Don't you want me to speak at all?

QUENTIN: That's ridiculous, Louise, why do you—

LOUISE: Because the moment I begin to assert myself it seems to threaten you. I don't think you *want* me to be happy.

QUENTIN—*there is a basic concession made by his tone of admitted bewilderment*: I tell you the truth, Louise—I don't think I feel very sure of myself any more. I feel sometimes that I don't see reality at all. I'm glad I took on Lou, but it only hit me lately that no respectable lawyer would touch him. It's like some unseen web of connection between people is simply not there. And I always relied on it, somehow; I never quite believed that people could be so easily disposed of. And it's larger than the political question. I think it's got me a little scared.

LOUISE, *with a wish for his sympathy, not accusing*: Well then, you must know how I felt when I found that letter in your suit.

QUENTIN—*he turns to her, aware*: I didn't do that to dispose of you, Louise.

> *She does not reply.*

I thought we'd settled about that girl.

> *She still does not reply.*

You mean you think I'm still . . .

LOUISE: I don't know what you're doing.

QUENTIN, *astounded*: What do you mean, you don't know?

LOUISE, *directly at him*: I said I don't know! I thought you told the truth about that other girl years ago, but after what happened again this spring—I don't know anything.

QUENTIN—*pause*: Tell me something; until this party the other night—in fact this whole year—I thought you seemed much happier. You were, weren't you?

LOUISE: Quentin, aren't you aware I've simply been staying out of your way this year?

QUENTIN, *amazed, frightened for his sense of reality*: Staying out of my way!

LOUISE: Well, can you remember one thing I've said about myself this year?

QUENTIN, *angrily, still amazed*: I swear to God, Louise, I thought we were building something till the other night!

LOUISE: But why?

QUENTIN: Well, I can't give you a bill of particulars, but it seems pretty obvious I've been trying like hell to show what I think of you. You've seen that, haven't you?

LOUISE: Quentin, you are full of resentment; you think I'm blind?

QUENTIN: What I resent is being forever on trial, Louise. Are you an innocent bystander here? I keep waiting for some contribution you might have made to what I did, and I resent not hearing it.

LOUISE: I said I did contribute; I demanded nothing for much too long.

QUENTIN: You mean the summer before last you didn't come to me and say that if I didn't change you would divorce me?

LOUISE: I never said I was *planning* a—

QUENTIN: You said if it came down to it you would divorce me —that's not a contribution?

LOUISE: Well, it certainly ought not send a man out to play doctor with the first girl he could lay his hands on!

QUENTIN: How much shame do you want me to feel? I hate what I did. But I think I've explained it—I felt like nothing; I shouldn't have, but I did, and I took the only means I knew to—

LOUISE: This is exactly what I mean, Quentin—you are still defending it. Right now.

> *He is stopped by this truth.*

And I know it, Quentin.

QUENTIN: And you're . . . not at all to blame, heh?

LOUISE: But how?

QUENTIN: Well, for example . . . you never turn your back on me in bed?

LOUISE: I never turned my—

QUENTIN: You have turned your back on me in bed, Louise. I am not insane!

LOUISE: Well what do you expect? Silent, cold, you lay your hand on me?

QUENTIN, *fallen*: Well, I . . . I'm not very demonstrative, I guess.

Slight pause. He throws himself on her compassion.

Louise . . . I worry about you all day. And all night.

LOUISE—*it is something, but not enough*: Well, you've got a child; I'm sure that worries you.

QUENTIN, *deeply hurt*: Is that all?

LOUISE, *with intense reasonableness*: Look, Quentin, it all comes down to a very simple thing; you want a woman to provide an . . . atmosphere, in which there are never any issues, and you'll fly around in a constant bath of praise . . .

QUENTIN: Well I wouldn't mind a little praise, what's wrong with praise?

LOUISE: Quentin, I am not a praise machine! I am not a blur and I am not your mother! I am a separate person!

QUENTIN—*he stares at her, and what lies beyond her*: I see that now.

LOUISE: It's no crime! Not if you're adult and grown-up.

QUENTIN, *quietly*: I guess not. But it bewilders me. In fact, I got the same idea when I realized that Lou had gone from one of his former students to another and none would take him . . .

LOUISE: What's Lou got to do with it? I think it's admirable that you . . .

QUENTIN: Yes, but I am doing what you call an admirable thing because I can't bear to be a separate person! I think so. I really don't want to be known as a Red lawyer; and I really don't want the newspapers to eat me alive; and if it came down to it, Lou could defend himself. But when that decent, broken man who never wanted anything but the good of the world, sits across my desk . . . I don't know how to say that my interests are no longer the same as his, and that if he doesn't change I consign him to hell because we are separate persons.

LOUISE: You are completely confused! Lou's case has nothing—

QUENTIN, *grasping for his thought*: I am telling you my confusion! I think Mickey also became a separate person.

LOUISE: You're incredible!

QUENTIN: I think of my mother, I think she also became—

LOUISE: Are you identifying *me* with—

QUENTIN: Louise, I am asking you to explain this to me because this is when I go blind! When you've finally become a separate person, what the hell is there?

LOUISE, *with a certain unsteady pride*: Maturity.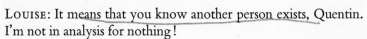

QUENTIN: I don't know what that means.

LOUISE: It means that you know another person exists, Quentin. I'm not in analysis for nothing!

QUENTIN, *questing*: It's probably the symptom of a typical case of some kind, but I swear, Louise—if you would just once, of your own will, as right as you are—if you would come to me and say that something, something important was your fault and that you were sorry . . . it would help.

> *In her pride she is silent, in her refusal to be brought down again.*

Louise?

LOUISE: Good God! What an idiot!

> *She begins to weep helplessly for her life, and vanishes. Light rises on a park bench with the sound of traffic. A young Negro hurries past, neat, wearing sunglasses, on the lookout, halts to flick dust off his shined shoes, goes on. An old woman in shapeless dress carries a shopping bag and a parrot in a cage across, limping. Quentin strolls on and sits on the bench, briefcase on his lap.*

QUENTIN: How few the days are that hold the mind in place; like a tapestry hanging on four or five hooks. Especially the day you stop becoming; the day you merely are. I suppose it's when the principles dissolve, and instead of the general gray of what ought to be you begin to see what is. Even the bench by the park seems alive, having held so many actual men. The word "Now" is like a bomb through the window, and it ticks.

> *The old woman recrosses with the parrot.*

Now a woman takes a parrot for a walk. Everything suddenly has consequences; she probably worries what will happen to it when she's gone.

> *A plain girl in tweeds passes, reading a paperback.*

And how brave a homely woman has to be! How disciplined of her, not to set fire to the museum of art.

The Negro passes, flicking dust off his shoe, comes to Quentin demanding a light for his cigarette. Quentin lights it.

And how does he keep so neat, and the bathroom on another floor? He must be furious when he shaves.

The Negro sees his girl upstage, walks off with her.

And whatever made me think that at the end of the day, I absolutely had to go home? You understand? That day when, suddenly, nothing whatsoever is ordained. Only . . . "Now," ticking away.

Maggie appears, looking about for someone.

Now there's a truth; symmetrical, lovely skin, undeniable.

MAGGIE: S'uze me, did you see a man with a big dog?

QUENTIN: No. But I saw a woman with a little bird.

MAGGIE: No, that's not him. Is this the bus stop?

QUENTIN: Ya, the sign says . . .

MAGGIE—*sits beside him*: I was standing over there and a man came with this big dog and just put the leash in my hand and walked away. So I started to go after him but the dog wouldn't move. And then this other man came and took the leash and went away. But I don't think it's really his dog. I think it's the first man's dog.

QUENTIN: But he obviously doesn't want it.

MAGGIE: But maybe he wanted for me to have it. I think the other man just saw it happening and figured he could get a free dog.

QUENTIN: Well, you want the dog?

MAGGIE: How could I keep a dog? I don't even think they allow dogs where I live. They might, but I never saw any dog. Although I'm not there much. What bus is this?

QUENTIN: Fifth Avenue. This is the downtown side. Where did you want to go?

MAGGIE—*thinks*: Well, I could go there.

QUENTIN: Where?

MAGGIE: Downtown.

QUENTIN: Lot of funny things go on, don't they?

MAGGIE: Well, he probably figured I would like a dog. Whereas I would if I had a way to keep it, but I don't even have a refrigerator.

QUENTIN: Yes. *Pause.* I guess he thought you had a refrigerator; that must be it.

> *She shrugs. Pause. He looks at her as she watches for the bus. He has no more to say. Louise lights up.*

LOUISE: You don't talk to any woman—not like a *woman*! You think reading your brief is *talking* to me?

> *She goes dark. In tension Quentin leans forward, arms resting on his knees. He looks at Maggie again. Anonymous men appear, lounge about, eying her.*

QUENTIN, *with an effort*: What do you do?

MAGGIE, *as though he should know*: On the switchboard.

QUENTIN: Oh, telephone operator?

MAGGIE—*laughs*: Don't you remember me?

QUENTIN, *surprised*: Me?

MAGGIE: I always sort of nod to you every morning through the window.

QUENTIN—*an instant*: Oh. In the reception room!

MAGGIE: Sure!

QUENTIN: What's your name?

MAGGIE: Maggie.

QUENTIN: Of course! You get my numbers sometimes.

MAGGIE: Did you think I just came up and started talking to you?

QUENTIN: I had no idea.

MAGGIE—*laughs*: Well what must you have thought!

QUENTIN: I didn't know what to think.

MAGGIE: I guess it's that you never saw me altogether. I mean just my head through that little window.

QUENTIN: Yes. Well, it's nice to meet all of you, finally.

MAGGIE—*laughs*: You go back to work again tonight?

QUENTIN: No, I'm just resting for a few minutes.

MAGGIE, *with a sense of his loneliness*: Oh.

> *She looks idly about. He glances down her body.*

QUENTIN: It's a pity you have to sit behind that little window.

> *She laughs, gratefully. Her eye catches something.*

MAGGIE, *rising*: Is that my bus down there?

QUENTIN: I'm not really sure where you want to go.

> *A man appears, eyes her, glances up toward the bus, back to her, staring.*

MAGGIE: I wanted to find one of those discount stores; I just bought a phonograph but I only have one record. I'll see you!

> *She is half-backing off toward the man.*

MAN: There's one on Twenty-seventh and Sixth Avenue.

MAGGIE, *turning, surprised*: Oh, thanks!

QUENTIN, *standing; moving toward her as though not to lose her to the man*: There's a record store around the corner, you know.

MAGGIE: But is it discount?

QUENTIN: Well they all discount—

MAN, *slipping his hand under her arm*: What, ten per cent? Come on, honey, I'll get you easy fifty off.

MAGGIE, *moving off on his arm*: Really? But Perry Sullivan?

MAN: Look, I'll give it to you—I'll give you two records! Come on!

MAGGIE—*she halts, suddenly aware; disengages her arm, backs*: S'uze me, I ... I ... forgot something.

MAN, *lathering*: Look, I'll give you ten records. *Calls off*. Hold that door! *Grabs her*. Come on!

QUENTIN, *moving toward him*: Hey!

MAN, *letting her go—to Quentin*: Ah, get lost! *He rushes off*. Hold it, hold the door!

> *Quentin watches the "bus" go by, then turns to her. She is absorbed in arranging her hair—but with a strangely doughy expression, removed.*

QUENTIN: I'm sorry, I thought you knew him.

MAGGIE: No. I never saw him.

QUENTIN: Well . . . what were you going with him for?

MAGGIE: Well he said he knew a store.

QUENTIN—*mystified, intrigued, looks at her, then nods inconclusively*: Oh.

MAGGIE: Where's the one you're talking about?

QUENTIN: I'll have to think a minute. Let's see . . .

MAGGIE: Could I sit with you? While you're thinking?

QUENTIN: Sure.

> *They return to the bench. He waits till she is seated; she is aware of the politeness, glances at him as he sits. Then she looks at him fully, for some reason amazed.*

That happen to you very often?

MAGGIE: Pretty often.

> *It is impossible to tell if she likes it or not.*

QUENTIN: It's because you talk to them.

MAGGIE: But they talk to me, so I have to answer.

QUENTIN: Not if they're rude.

MAGGIE: But if they talk to me . . .

QUENTIN: Just turn your back.

MAGGIE—*she thinks about that, and indecisively*: Oh, okay. *As though remotely aware of another world, his world*: . . . Thanks, though . . . for stopping it.

QUENTIN: Well, anybody would.

MAGGIE: No, they laugh. It's a joke to them. *She laughs in pain. Slight pause.* You . . . going to rest here very long?

QUENTIN: Just a few minutes. I'm on my way home. I never did this before.

MAGGIE: Oh! You look like you always did.

QUENTIN: Why?

MAGGIE: I don't know. You look like you could sit for hours, under these trees . . . just thinking.

QUENTIN: No. I usually go right home. *Grinning.* I've always gone right home.

MAGGIE—*she absorbs this*: Oh. *Coming awake*: See, I'm still paying for the phonograph, whereas they don't sell records on time, you know.

QUENTIN: They're afraid they'll wear out, I guess.

MAGGIE: Oh, that must be it! I always wondered. Cause you *can* get phonographs. How'd you know that?

QUENTIN: I don't. I'm just guessing.

MAGGIE: It sounds true, though. *Laughs.* I can never guess those things! I don't know why they do anything half the time! *She laughs more deeply. He does.* I had about ten or twenty records in Washington, but my friend got sick, and I had to leave. Although maybe they're still there.

QUENTIN: Well, if you still have the apartment . . .

MAGGIE: I'm not sure I do. I got a letter from them couple months ago, the Real Estate. *Pause. Thinks.* I better open it. He lived right over there on Park Avenue.

QUENTIN: Oh. Is he better?

MAGGIE: He died. *Tears come into her eyes.*

QUENTIN, *entirely perplexed*: When was this?

MAGGIE: Friday. Remember they closed the office for the day?

QUENTIN: You mean—*Astounded*—Judge Cruse?

MAGGIE: Ya.

QUENTIN, *with lingering surprise*: Oh, I didn't know that you . . . He was a great lawyer. And a great judge, too.

MAGGIE, *rubbing tears*: He was very nice to me.

QUENTIN: I was at the funeral; I didn't see you, though.

MAGGIE, *with difficulty against her tears*: His wife wouldn't let me come. But I got into the hospital before he died. But as soon as I opened the door of his room the family pushed me out and . . . I

could hear him calling, "Maggie! Maggie!" *Pause.* They kept trying to offer me a thousand dollars. But I told them, I don't want anything, I just wanted to say good-by to him!

She opens her purse, takes out an office envelope, opens it.

I have a little of the dirt. See? That's from his grave. His chauffeur drove me out—Alexander.

QUENTIN—*looks at the dirt, at her face*: Did he leave you very much?

MAGGIE: No, he didn't leave me anything.

She puts the envelope back, closes the purse, stares.

QUENTIN: Did you love him very much?

MAGGIE: No. But he was very nice. In fact, a couple of times I really left him.

QUENTIN: Why didn't you altogether?

MAGGIE: He didn't want me to.

QUENTIN: Oh. *Pause.* So what are you going to do now?

MAGGIE: I'd love to get that record if I knew where they had a discount.

QUENTIN: No, I mean in general.

MAGGIE: Why, they going to fire me now?

QUENTIN: Oh, I wouldn't know about that.

MAGGIE: Although I'm not worried, whereas I can always go back to hair.

QUENTIN: To where?

MAGGIE: I used to demonstrate hair preparations. *Laughs, squirts her hair with an imaginary bottle.* You know, in department stores? I was traveling even, they sent me to Boston and New Orleans and all over. *Tilting her head under his chin*: It's because I have very thick hair, you see? I have my mother's hair. And it's not broken. You notice I have no broken hair? Most women's hair is broken. Here, feel it, feel how— *She has lifted his hand to her head, and suddenly lets go of it.* Oh, s'uze me!

QUENTIN: That's all right.

MAGGIE: I just thought you might want to feel it.

QUENTIN: Sure.

MAGGIE: Go ahead. I mean if you want to.

> *She leans her head to him again. He touches the top of her head.*

QUENTIN: It is, ya! Very soft.

MAGGIE, *proudly*: I once went from page boy to bouffant in less than ten minutes!

QUENTIN: What made you quit?

MAGGIE—*the dough comes into her eyes again*: They start sending me to conventions and all. You're supposed to entertain, you see.

QUENTIN: Oh, yes.

MAGGIE: There were parts of it I didn't like any more.

> *A long moment. A student goes by, reading. He looks up from his book, shyly glances at her, goes on reading. She laughs.*

Aren't they sweet when they look up from their books!

> *She turns to him with a laugh. He looks at her warmly, smiling.*

S'uze me I put your hand on my head.

QUENTIN: Oh, that's all right. . . . I'm not *that* bad. *He laughs softly, embarrassed.*

MAGGIE: You're not bad.

QUENTIN: I don't mean bad, I mean . . . shy.

MAGGIE: It's not bad to be shy. *She gives him a long look, absorbed.* I mean . . . if that's the way you are.

QUENTIN: I guess I am, then.

> *Pause. They look at each other.*

You're very beautiful, Maggie.

> *She smiles, straightens as though his words had entered her.*

And I wish you knew how to take care of yourself.

MAGGIE: Oh . . . *Holding out a ripped seam in her dress*: I got this torn on the bus this morning. I'm going to sew it home.

QUENTIN: I don't mean that.

> *She meets his eyes again—she looks chastised.*

Not that I'm criticizing you. I'm not at all. Not in the slightest.
You understand?

> *She nods, absorbed in his face. He stands.*

I've got to go now.

> *She stands, staring at him, giving herself. He sees this. His hand
> moves, but it becomes a handshake.*

You could look up record stores in the phone book.

MAGGIE: I think I'll take a walk in the park.

QUENTIN: You shouldn't. It's getting dark.

MAGGIE: But it's beautiful at night. I slept there one night when
it was hot in my room.

QUENTIN: God, you don't want to do that! I know this park.
Most of the animals are not in the zoo.

MAGGIE: Okay. I'll get a record, then. *She backs a step.* S'uze me
about my hair if I embarrassed you.

QUENTIN—*laughs*: You didn't.

MAGGIE—*backing to leave, she touches the top of her head*: It's just that
it's not broken.

> *He nods. She halts some yards away, holds out her torn seam.*

I'm going to sew this home.

> *He nods. She indicates the park, upstage.*

I didn't *mean* to sleep there. I just fell asleep.

> *Two young guys appear, pass Quentin, slow as they pass her,
> and halt in the far periphery of the light, waiting for her.*

QUENTIN: I understand.

MAGGIE: Well . . . see you! *Laughs.* If they don't fire me!

QUENTIN: 'By.

> *She passes the two men, who walk step for step behind her,
> whispering in her ear together. She doesn't turn or answer but
> shows no surprise.*

QUENTIN—*in anguish he hurries after her*: Maggie! *He catches her arm
and brings her clear of the men, takes a bill from his pocket.* Here, why

don't you take a cab? It's on me. Go ahead, there's one right there. *Points and whistles.* Go on, grab it!

MAGGIE, *backing in the opposite direction from the waiting men*: Where . . . where will I tell him to go but?

QUENTIN: Just cruise in the forties—you've got enough there.

MAGGIE: Okay, 'by! *Backing out*: You . . . you just going to rest more?

QUENTIN: I don't know.

MAGGIE, *wondrously*: Golly, that's nice!

> *She hurries off. He stands staring after her. Likewise, the men watch the "cab" going by, then walk off.*

> *Lights rise on Louise reading in a chair. Quentin, clasping his briefcase behind his back, walks slowly into the area, stands a few yards from her, staring at her. She remains unaware of him, reading and smoking.*

QUENTIN: Yes. She has legs, breasts, mouth, eyes. How wonderful—a woman of my own! What a miracle! In my own house!

> *He walks to her, bends and kisses her. She looks up at him surprised, perplexed.*

Hi.

> *She keeps looking up at him, aware of some sealike opening in the world.*

What's the matter?

> *She still doesn't speak.*

Well, what's the matter?

LOUISE: Nothing.

> *She returns to her book. Mystified, disappointed, he stands watching, then opens his briefcase and begins taking out papers.*

Close the door if you're going to type.

QUENTIN: I always do.

LOUISE: Not always.

QUENTIN: Almost always.

> *He almost laughs, he feels loose, but she won't be amused, and returns again to her book. He starts for the bedroom, halts.*

How about eating out tomorrow night? Before the parents' meeting?

LOUISE: What parents' meeting?

QUENTIN: The school.

LOUISE: That was tonight.

QUENTIN, *shocked*: Really?

LOUISE: Of course. I just got back.

QUENTIN: Why didn't you remind me when I called today?

LOUISE: You knew it as well as I.

QUENTIN: But you know I often forget those things. I told you I wanted to talk to her teacher.

LOUISE, *a little more sharply*: People do what they want to do, Quentin.

QUENTIN: But Louise, I was talking to you at three o'clock this afternoon . . .

LOUISE—*an unwilling shout*: Because you said you had to work tonight!

> *She glares at him meaningfully; returns to her book. He stands, alarmed.*

QUENTIN: I didn't work.

LOUISE, *keeping to her book*: *I* know you didn't work.

QUENTIN, *surprised*: How did you know?

LOUISE: Well for one thing, Max called here at seven-thirty.

QUENTIN: Max? What for?

LOUISE: Apparently the whole executive committee was in his office waiting to meet with you tonight.

> *His hand goes to his head; open alarm shows on his face.*

He called three times, as a matter of fact.

QUENTIN: I forgot all about it! *He hurries to the phone, stops.* How is that possible? It completely—

LOUISE: Well they wouldn't be there any more now. *Pointedly:* It's ten-thirty.

QUENTIN: My God, I—How could I do that? What's his home number?

LOUISE: The book is in the bedroom.

QUENTIN: We were supposed to discuss my handling Lou's case. DeVries stayed in town tonight just to . . . settle everything. And I go and walk out as though . . . nothing . . . *Breaks off. Picks up phone.* What's Max's number, Murray Hill 3 . . . what is it?

LOUISE: The book is next to the bed.

QUENTIN: You remember it, Murray Hill 3, something.

LOUISE: It's in the book.

Pause. He looks at her. Puzzled.

QUENTIN: What are you doing?

LOUISE: I'm saying the book is in the bedroom.

QUENTIN—*slams the phone down, and, as much in fright as in anger*: But you remember his number!

LOUISE: I'm not the keeper of your phone numbers. You can remember them just as well as I.

QUENTIN: Oh, I see. *Nods ironically, starts out.*

LOUISE: Please don't use that phone, you'll wake her up.

QUENTIN—*turns*: I had no intention of calling in there.

LOUISE: I thought you might want to be private.

QUENTIN: There's nothing private about this. This concerns you as much as me. The food in your mouth and the clothes on your back.

LOUISE: Really! When did you start thinking of us?

QUENTIN: The meeting was called to decide whether I should separate from the firm until Lou's case is over—or permanently, for all I know.

Quentin goes toward the phone. She stands staring in growing fright.

Murray Hill 3 . . .

He picks it up, dials one digit.

LOUISE, *much against her will*: That's the old number.

QUENTIN: Murray Hill 3-4598.

LOUISE: It's been changed. *A moment; and finally*: Cortland 7-7098.

QUENTIN—*she is not facing him; he senses what he thinks is victory*: Thanks.

> *Starts again to dial, puts down the phone. She sits; there is an admission of the faintest sort of failing in her.*

I don't know what to say to him.

> *She is silent.*

We arranged for everybody to come back after dinner. It'll sound idiotic that I forgot about it.

LOUISE: You were probably frightened.

QUENTIN: But I made notes all afternoon about what I would say tonight! It's incredible!

LOUISE, *with an over-meaning*: You probably don't realize how frightened you are.

QUENTIN: I guess I don't. He said a dreadful thing today—Max. He was trying to argue me into dropping Lou and I said, "The law is the law; we can't adopt some new behavior just because there's hysteria in the country." I thought it was a perfectly ordinary thing to say but he—he's never looked at me that way—like we were suddenly standing on two distant mountains; and he said, "I don't know of any hysteria. Not in this office."

LOUISE, *without rancor*: But why does all that surprise you?

QUENTIN—*slight pause*: I don't understand exactly what you're getting at.

LOUISE: Simply that there are some issues you have to face. You tend to make relatives out of people. Max is not your father, or your brother, or anything but a very important lawyer with his own interests. He's not going to endanger his whole firm to defend a Communist. I don't know how you got that illusion.

QUENTIN: You mean—

LOUISE: I mean you can't have everything; if you feel this strongly about Lou you probably will have to resign.

QUENTIN—*pause*: You think I should?

LOUISE: That depends on how deeply you feel about Lou.

QUENTIN: I'm trying to determine that; I don't know for sure. What do you think?

LOUISE, *in anguish*: It's not my decision, Quentin.

QUENTIN, *puzzled and surprised*: But aren't you involved?

LOUISE: Of course I'm involved.

QUENTIN, *genuinely foxed*: Is it that you're not sure of how you feel?

LOUISE: I know how I feel but it is not my decision.

QUENTIN: I'm only curious how you—

LOUISE: You? Curious about me?

QUENTIN: Oh. We're not talking about what we're talking about, are we?

LOUISE, *nodding in emphasis*: You have to decide what you feel about a certain human being. For once in your life. And then maybe you'll decide what you feel about other human beings. Clearly and decisively.

QUENTIN: In other words . . . where was I tonight.

LOUISE: I don't care where you were tonight.

QUENTIN—*pause*: I sat by the park for a while. And this is what I thought. I don't sleep with other women, but I think I behave as though I do.

She is listening. He sees it, is enlivened by hope.

Maybe I invite your suspicion on myself in order to . . . to come down off some bench, to stop judging others so perfectly. Because I do judge, and harshly, too—when the fact is I'm bewildered. I even wonder if I left that letter for you to read . . . about that girl . . . in order to . . . somehow join the condemned; in some way to start being real. Can you understand that?

LOUISE: But . . . *She is digging in her heels against being taken.* Why should you be condemned if you're not still doing anything?

QUENTIN, *uneasily again*: But don't you continue to feel ashamed for something you've done in the past? You can understand that, can't you?

LOUISE: I don't do things I'll be ashamed of.

QUENTIN, *now astonished, and moving toward anger*: Really and truly?

LOUISE—*starts to rise*: I'm going to bed.

QUENTIN: I have to say it, Louise; whenever our conversations verge on you, they end. You say you want to talk, but is it only about my sins?

LOUISE: Now you listen here! You've been "at the office" one night a week since last winter. It's not my forgiveness you want, it's the end of this marriage! But you haven't the courage to say so!

QUENTIN: All right, then. *Against his own trepidation, striving for a clear conscience:* I think I won't be ashamed either. I met a girl to-night. Just happened to come by, one of the phone operators in the office. I probably shouldn't tell you this either, but I will.

> *She sits, slowly.*

Quite stupid, silly kid. Sleeps in the park, her dress is ripped; she said some ridiculous things, but one thing struck me, she wasn't defending anything, upholding anything, or accusing—she was just *there*, like a tree or a cat. And I felt strangely abstract beside her. And I saw that we are killing one another with abstractions. I'm defending Lou because I love him, yet the society transforms that love into a kind of treason, what they call an issue, and I end up suspect and hated. Why can't we speak below the "issues"—with our real uncertainty? I walked in just now—and I had a tremendous wish to come out—to you. And you to me. It sounds absurd that this city is full of people rushing to meet one another, Louise. This city is full of lovers. . . .

LOUISE: And what did she say?

QUENTIN: I guess I shouldn't have told you about it.

LOUISE: Why not?

QUENTIN: Louise, I don't know what's permissible to say any more.

LOUISE—*nods*: You don't know how much to hide.

QUENTIN—*he angers*: All right, let's not hide anything; it would have been easy to make love to her.

> *Louise reddens, stiffens.*

And I didn't because I thought of you, and in a new way . . . like a stranger I had never gotten to know. And by some miracle you were waiting for me, in my own home. I came into this room, Louise, full of love . . .

LOUISE: What do you want, my congratulations? You expect me to sit here and enjoy your latest conquest? You take me for a Lesbian?

QUENTIN, *perplexed*: What's a Lesbian got to do with . . .

LOUISE: Ask your friend with the torn dress. You don't imagine a real woman goes to bed with any man who happens to come along? Or that a real man goes to bed with every woman who'll have him? Especially a slut, which she obviously is?

QUENTIN: How do you know she's a—

LOUISE—*laughs*: Oh, excuse me, I didn't mean to insult her! You're unbelievable! Supposing I came home and told you I'd met a man—a man on the street I wanted to go to bed with . . .

> *He hangs his head, defeated.*

because he made the city seem full of lovers. What would you feel? Overjoyed for my discovery?

QUENTIN—*pause; struck*: I understand. I'm sorry. I guess it would anger me too. *Slight pause.* But if you came to me with such a thing, I think I would see that you were struggling. And I would ask myself—maybe I'd even be brave enough to ask you—how *I* had failed.

LOUISE: Well, you've given me notice; I get the message.

> *She starts out.*

QUENTIN: Louise, don't you ever doubt yourself?

> *She slows, but does not turn.*

Is it enough to prove a case, to even win it—*Shouts*—when we are dying?

LOUISE—*turns in full possession*: I'm not dying. I'm not the one who

end but I hated the danger in it for myself, and he saw through my faithfulness; and he was not telling me what a friend I was, he was praying I would be—"Please be my friend, Quentin," is what he was saying to me, "I am drowning, throw me a rope!" Because I wanted out, to be a good American again, kosher again—and he saw it, and proved it in the joy . . . the joy . . . the joy I felt now that my danger had spilled out on the subway track! So it is not bizarre to me. . . .

The tower blazes into life, and he walks with his eyes up.

Holga appears with flowers.

This is not some crazy aberration of human nature to me. I can easily see the perfectly normal contractors and their cigars; the carpenters, plumbers, sitting at their ease over lunch pails, I can see them laying the pipes to run the blood out of this mansion; good fathers, devoted sons, grateful that someone else will die, not they. And how can one understand that, if one is innocent; if somewhere in the soul there is no accomplice . . .

The tower fades, Holga too. Louise brightens in light where she was standing before.

. . . of that joy, that joy, that joy when a burden dies . . .

He moves back into the "room."

. . . and leaves you safe?

Maggie's breathing is heard.

MAGGIE: Quentin?

He turns in pain from it, comes to a halt on one side of the sheets and pillow lying on the floor. Louise is on the other side. He looks down at the pile.

QUENTIN: I've got to sleep; I'm very tired.

He bends to pick up the sheets. A split second later she starts to. And while he is still reaching down . . .

LOUISE, *with great difficulty:* I . . .

He stands with the sheets in hand, the pillow still on the floor; now he is attending her, sensing a confession.

I've always been proud you took Lou's case.

He barely nods, waiting.

It was . . .

She picks up the pillow.

courageous.

She stands there with the pillow, not fully looking at him.

QUENTIN: I'm glad you feel that way.

But he makes no move. The seconds are ticking by. Neither can let down his demand for apology, for grace. With difficulty:

And that you told me. Thanks.

LOUISE: You are honest—that way. I've often told you.

QUENTIN: Recently?

LOUISE—*bridles, hands him the pillow*: Good night.

He takes the pillow; she starts away, and he feels the unwilling-ness with which she leaves.

QUENTIN: Louise, if there's one thing I've been trying to do it's to be honest with you.

LOUISE: No. You've been trying to arrange things, that's all—to keep the home fires burning and see the world at the same time.

QUENTIN: So that all I am is deceptive, and cunning.

LOUISE: Not all, but mostly.

QUENTIN: And there is no struggle. There is no pain. There is no struggle to find a way back to you?

LOUISE: That isn't the struggle.

QUENTIN: Then what are you doing here?

LOUISE: I . . .

QUENTIN: What the hell are you compromising yourself for if you're so goddamned honest?

On the line he starts a frustrated clench-fisted move toward her and she backs away, terrified, and strangely alive. Her look takes note of the aborted violence and she is very straight and yet ready to flee.

LOUISE: I've been waiting for the struggle to begin.

He is dumbstruck—by her sincerity, her adamance. With a straight look at him, she turns and goes out.

QUENTIN, *alone, and to himself*: Good God, can there be more? Can there be worse?

> *Turning to the Listener:*

See, that's what's incredible to me—three years more! What did I expect to save us? Suddenly, God knows why, she'd hold out her hand and I hold out mine, and laugh, laugh it all away, laugh it all back to . . . her dear, honest face looking up to mine. . . .

> *Breaks off, staring.*

Back to some hidden, everlasting smile that saves. That's maybe why I came; I think I still believe it. That underneath we're all profoundly friends! I can't believe this world; all this hatred isn't real to me!

> *Turns back to his "living room," and the sheets.*

To bed down like a dog in my living room, how can that be necessary? Then go in to her, open your heart, confess the lechery, the mystery of women, say it all . . . the truth must save!

> *He has moved toward where she exited, now halts.*

But I did that. So the truth, after all, may merely be murderous? The truth killed Lou; destroyed Mickey. Then what else is there? A workable lie? Maybe there is only one sin, to destroy your own credibility. Strength comes from a clear conscience or a dead one. Not to see one's own evil—there's power! And rightness too! So kill conscience. Kill it.

> *Glancing toward her exit.*

Know all, admit nothing, shave closely, remember birthdays, open car doors, pursue Louise not with truth but with attention. Be uncertain on your own time, in bed be absolute. And thus, be a man . . . and join the world.

> *Reflectively he throws the sheet open on the couch, then stops.*

And in the morning, a dagger in that dear little daughter's heart!

> *Flinging it toward Louise's exit.*

Bitch!

> *Sits.*

I'll say I have a cold. Didn't want to give it to Mommy.

> *With disgust.*

Pah! Papapapapa.

Sniffs, tries to talk through his nose.

Got a cold in my dose, baby girl . . .

He groans. Pause. He stares; stalemate. A jet plane is heard. An airport porter appears, unloads two bags from a rolling cart as Holga, dressed for travel, appears opening her purse, tipping him, and now looking about for Quentin. A distant jet roars in take-off. Quentin glances at his watch, and, coming down to the chair:

Six o'clock, Idlewild.

Now he glances at Holga, who is still looking about him as in a crowd, and speaks to the Listener.

It's that the evidence is bad for promises. But how do you touch the world without a promise? And yet, I mustn't forget the way I wake; I open up my eyes each morning like a boy, even now, even now! That's as true as anything I know, but where's the evidence? Or is it simply that my heart still beats? . . . Certainly, go ahead.

He smiles and sits, following the departing Listener with his eyes; A light moves upstage, going away. He talks upstage.

You don't mind my staying? Good. I'd like to settle this. Although actually, I—*Laughs*—only came by to say hello.

He turns front. The Listener's light is gone. Alone now, he stares ahead, a different kind of relaxation on him. From the darkness high on the upper level, the sucking breathing is heard; light dimly shows Maggie, her back to us, sitting up in the "bed."

MAGGIE: Quentin?

QUENTIN, *in agony*: I'll get to it, honey.

He closes his eyes.

I'll get to it.

He stands, and as though wandering in a room he moves at random, puts a cigarette in his mouth, and strikes sparks from his lighter as darkness covers him.

Act Two

*The stage is dark. A spark is seen; a flame fires up. When the
stage illuminates, Quentin is discovered lighting his cigarette—no
time has passed. He continues to await the Listener's return, and
walks a few steps in thought and as he does a jet plane is heard,
and the garbled airport announcer's voice: ". . . from Frankfurt
is now unloading at gate nine, passengers will please . . ." It
becomes a watery garble and at the same moment Holga, beauti-
fully dressed, walks onto the upper level with an airport porter,
who leaves her bags and goes. She looks about as in a crowd—
then, seeing "Quentin," stands on tiptoe and waves.*

HOLGA: Quentin! Here! Here!

She opens her arms as he evidently approaches.

Hello!

*She is gone as Louise rushes on from another point, a ribbon in
her hair, a surgical mask hanging from her neck, a lab technician's
smock open to show her sweater and long skirt of the thirties. A
hospital attendant is mopping the floor behind her. She sees
"Quentin."*

LOUISE: Hello! I just got my final grades! I got an A on that paper
you wrote! Ya—the one on Roosevelt. I'm a Master! *Laughs.* And
guess what Halliday said. That my style has immeasurably im-
proved! *Laughs; and now she walks with "him."* If it wasn't for the
mop I'd think you were an intern in that uniform; you look well
in white. *Her face falls; she halts.* Oh! Then when would you be
leaving? . . . No, I'm glad, I always heard Columbia Law was the

best. *Shyly*: Actually, I could try some labs in New York, it'd be cheaper if I lived at home. . . . Well, then, I'd look for something else; anyway there are more bacteriologists than bugs these days. *With dread and shyness*: Unless you wouldn't want me to be there. *She bursts into an adoring smile.* Okay! You want a malt later? I have some money, I just sold all my textbooks! Oop! *She stops abruptly, looking down at the floor.* I'm sorry! I forgot it was wet! See you!

> *With a happy wave of her hand she picks her way on tiptoe over a wet floor into darkness as a door is heard opening upstage and a light moves downstage, over the floor; Quentin turns toward the returning Listener and smiles.*

QUENTIN: Oh, that's all right, I didn't mind waiting. How much time do I have?

> *He looks at his watch, coming down to the chair. Maggie appears, above, in a lace wedding dress; Lucas, a designer, is on his knees finishing the vast hem. Carrie, a maid, stands by, holding gloves. Maggie is nervous, on the edge of life, looking into a "mirror."*

> *Quentin sits in the chair. He looks forward now, to speak.*

I, ah . . .

> *Lucas gets up and quickly goes as . . .*

MAGGIE, *in an ecstasy of fear and hope*: All right, Carrie, tell him to come in! *As though trying the angular words*: . . . My *husband*!

CARRIE, *walking a few steps to a point, halts*: You can see her now, Mister Quentin.

> *They are gone. He continues to the Listener.*

QUENTIN: I think I can be clearer now, it shouldn't take long. I am bewildered by the death of love. And my responsibility for it.

> *Holga appears again, looking about for him at the airport.*

This woman's on my side; I have no doubt of it. And I wouldn't want to outlive another accusation. Not hers. *He stands, agitated.* I suddenly wonder why I risk it again. Except . . . *Slight pause; he becomes still.* You ever felt you once saw yourself—absolutely true? I may have dreamed it, but I swear, I feel that somewhere along the line—with Maggie I think—for one split second I saw my life;

what I had done, what had been done to me, and even what I ought to do. And that vision sometimes hangs behind my head, blind now, bleached out like the moon in the morning; and if I could only let in some necessary darkness it would shine again. I think it had to do with power.

Felice appears, about to remove the bandage.

Maybe that's why she sticks in my mind; she brings some darkness. Some dreadful element of power. *He walks around her, peering.* . . . Well, that's power isn't it? To influence a girl to change her nose, her life? . . . It does, yes, it frightens me, and I wish to God . . .

FELICE, *raising her arm*: I'll always . . .

QUENTIN: . . . she'd stop blessing me! *He laughs uneasily, surprised at the force of his fear.* . . . Well, I suppose because there is a fraud involved; I have no such power.

Maggie suddenly appears in a "satin bed," talking into a phone.

MAGGIE, *with timid idolatry*: Hello? Is . . . How'd you know it's me? *Laughs.* You really remember me? Maggie? From that park that day? Well 'cause it's almost four years so I . . .

He comes away from her; she continues talking unheard. He halts near the chair. He glances toward a point where again Felice appears, raising her arm in blessing, and instantly disappears, and he speaks to the Listener.

QUENTIN: I do, yes, I see the similarity.

Laughter is heard as Holga appears at a "café table," an empty chair beside her.

HOLGA: I love the way you eat! You eat like a pasha, a grand duke!

QUENTIN—*looks toward her, and to Listener*: Yes, adored again! But . . . there is something different here.

As he moves toward Holga, he says to Listener:

Now keep me to my theme. I spoke of power.

He sits beside her. As he speaks now, Holga's aspect changes; she becomes moody, doesn't face him, seems hurt. And sitting beside her he tells the Listener:

We were in a café one afternoon in Salzburg, and quite suddenly,

I don't know why—it all seemed to be dying between us. And I saw it all happening again. You know that moment, when you begin desperately to talk about architecture?

HOLGA: Fifteen-thirty-five. The archbishop designed it himself.

QUENTIN: Beautiful.

HOLGA, *distantly*: Yes.

QUENTIN—*as though drawing on his courage, he suddenly turns to her*: Holga. I thought I noticed your pillow was wet this morning.

HOLGA: It really isn't anything important.

QUENTIN: There are no unimportant tears. *Takes her hand, smiles.* I know that much, anyway. Unless it doesn't concern me. Is it about the concentration camp?

She wipes her eyes, unhappy with herself.

Even during the day, sometimes, you seem about to weep.

HOLGA: I feel sometimes . . . *Breaks off, then*: . . . that I'm boring you.

Louise appears.

LOUISE: I am not all this uninteresting, Quentin!

Louise is gone.

HOLGA: I really think perhaps we've been together too much.

QUENTIN: Except, it's only been a few weeks.

HOLGA: But I may not be all that interesting.

Quentin stares at her, trying to join this with his lost vision, and in that mood he turns out to the Listener.

QUENTIN: The question is power, but I've lost the connection.

Louise appears brushing her hair.

Yes!

He springs up and circles Louise.

I tell you, there were times when she looked into the mirror and I saw she didn't like her face, and I wanted to step between her and what she saw. I felt guilty even for her face! But . . . that day . . .

He returns to the café table and slowly sits.

there was some new permission . . . not to take a certain blame. There was suddenly no blame at all but that . . . we're each entitled to . . . our own unhappiness.

HOLGA: I wish you'd believe me, Quentin; you have no duty here.

QUENTIN: Holga, I would go. But the truth is, I'd be looking for you tomorrow. I wouldn't know where the hell I thought I had to be. But there's truth in what you feel. I see it very clearly; the time does come when I feel I must go. Not toward anything, or away from you. But there is some freedom in the going. . . .

Mother appears, and she is raising her arm.

MOTHER: Darling, there is never a depression for great people! The first time I felt you move, I was standing on the beach at Rockaway. . . .

Quentin has gotten up from the chair, and, moving toward her:

QUENTIN: But power. Where is the—?

MOTHER: And I saw a star, and it got bright, and brighter, and brighter! And suddenly it fell, like some great man had died, and you were being pulled out of me to take his place, and be a light, a light in the world!

QUENTIN, *to Listener:* Why is there some . . . air of treachery in that?

FATHER, *suddenly appearing—to Mother:* What the hell are you talking about? We're just getting a business started again, I need him!

Quentin avidly turns from one to the other as they argue.

MOTHER: You've got Dan, you don't need him! He wants to try to get a job, go to college, maybe—

FATHER: He's got a job!

MOTHER: He means with pay! I don't want his young years going by. . . . He wants a life!

FATHER, *indicating Dan:* Why don't he "want a life"?

MOTHER: Because he's different!

FATHER: Because *he* knows what's *right*!

Indicating Mother and Quentin together:

You're two of a kind—what you "want"! Chrissake, when I was his age I was supporting six people!

He comes up to Quentin.

What are you, a stranger? *What are you?*

Quentin is peering into the revulsion of his Father's face. And he turns toward Holga in the café and back to Father.

QUENTIN: Yes, I felt a power in the going . . . and treason in it. . . . Because there's failure, and you turn your back on failure.

DAN: No, kid, don't feel that way. I just want to see him big again, but you go. I'll go back to school if things pick up.

QUENTIN, *peering at Dan*: Yes, good men stay . . . although they die there.

DAN, *indicating a book in his hand*: It's my Byron, I'll put it in your valise, and I've put in my new argyles, just don't wash them in hot water. And remember, kid, wherever you are . . .

Dan jumps onto a platform, calling. A passing train is heard.

. . . wherever you are this family's behind you! You buckle down, now. . . . I'll send you a list of books to read!

MAGGIE, *suddenly appearing on her bed; she is addressing an empty space at the foot*: But could I read them!

QUENTIN—*spins about in quick surprise*: Huh!

All the others are gone dark but he and Maggie.

MAGGIE: I mean what kind of books? 'Cause, see . . . I never really graduated high school. *She laughs nervously.* Although in Social Science he liked me so he let me keep the minutes. Except I didn't know what's a minute! *Laughs.* I like poetry, though.

QUENTIN—*breaks his stare at her, and quickly comes down to the Listener*: It's that I can't find myself in this vanity, any more. It's all contemptible! *He covers his face.*

MAGGIE, *enthralled, on the bed*: I can't hardly believe you came! Can you stay five minutes? I'm a singer now, see? In fact—*With a laugh at herself*—I'm in the top three. And for a long time I been wanting to tell you that . . . none of it would have happened to me if I hadn't met you that day.

QUENTIN: . . . Yes, I see the power she offered me; but I saw beyond it once, and there was some . . . salvation in it. . . . All right. I'll . . .

He turns to her, walking into her line of sight.

. . . try.

MAGGIE: I'm sorry if I sounded frightened on the phone but I didn't think you'd be in the office after midnight. *Laughs at herself nervously.* See, I only pretended to call you. Can you stay like five minutes?

QUENTIN, *backing into the chair*: Sure. Don't rush.

MAGGIE: That's what I mean, you know I'm rushing! Would you like a drink? Or a steak? They have two freezers here. Whereas my agent went to Jamaica, so I'm just staying here this week till I go to London Friday. It's the Palladium, like a big vaudeville house, and it's kind of an honor, but I'm a little scared to go.

QUENTIN: Why? I've heard you; you're marvelous. Especially . . .

He can't remember a title.

MAGGIE: No, I'm just flapping my wings yet. I mean if you ever heard like Ella Fitzgerald or one of those . . . But did you read what that *News* fellow wrote? He keeps my records in the frigerator, case they melt!

QUENTIN—*laughs with her*:—"Little Girl Blue"—it's very moving the way you do that.

MAGGIE, *surprised and pleased*: Really? 'Cause see, it's not I say to myself "I'm going to sound sexy," I just try to come *through* . . . like, in love or . . . *Laughs.* I really can't believe you're here!

QUENTIN: Why? I'm glad you called. I've often thought about you the last couple of years. All the great things happening to you gave me a secret satisfaction for some reason.

MAGGIE: Maybe 'cause you did it.

QUENTIN: Why do you say that?

MAGGIE: I don't know, just the way you looked at me . . . I didn't even have the nerve to go see an agent before that day.

QUENTIN: How did I look at you?

MAGGIE, *squinching up her shoulders, feeling for the mystery*: Like . . . out of your *self*. See, most people they . . . just look *at* you. I can't explain it! And the way you talked to me . . .

Louise appears.

LOUISE: You think reading your brief is talking to me?

And she is gone.

QUENTIN, *to Listener, of Louise*: Yes, I see that, but there was something more. And maybe power isn't quite the word . . .

MAGGIE: What did you mean . . . it gave you a secret satisfaction?

QUENTIN: Just that . . . like in the office, I'd hear people laughing that Maggie had the world at her feet. . . .

MAGGIE, *hurt, mystified*: They laughed!

QUENTIN: In a way.

MAGGIE, *in pain*: That's what I mean; I'm a joke to most people.

QUENTIN: No, it's that you say what you mean, Maggie. You don't seem to be upholding anything, or . . . You're not ashamed of what you are.

MAGGIE: W—what do you mean of what I am?

Louise appears; she is playing solitaire.

QUENTIN, *suddenly aware he has touched a nerve*: Well . . . that you love life, and . . . It's hard to define, I—

LOUISE: The word is tart. But what did it matter as long as she praised you?

QUENTIN, *to Listener, standing, and moving within Maggie's area*: But there's truth in it—I hadn't had a woman's praise, even a girl I'd laughed at with the others . . .

MAGGIE: But you didn't, did you?

He turns to her in agony; Louise vanishes.

Laugh at me?

QUENTIN: No.

He suddenly stands and cries out to Listener:

Fraud—from the first five minutes! . . . Because—I should have agreed she *was* a joke, a beautiful piece trying to take herself seriously! Why did I lie to her, play this cheap benefactor, this . . . What? *Listens, and now, unwillingly*: Yes, that's true too; she had; a strange, surprising honor.

> *He turns back to her.*

MAGGIE: Oh, hey? I just bought back two records I made!

QUENTIN: Bought them back how?

MAGGIE: Well, they're no good, just stupid rock-and-rolly stuff, and I start to think—*Laughs shyly*—maybe you'd turn on your radio, and I didn't want you to hear them. Is that crazy?

QUENTIN: No, but it's pretty unusual to care that much.

MAGGIE: I didn't used to, either. Honest.

QUENTIN, *mystified*: But I hardly said anything to you that day.

MAGGIE: Well, like—*Afraid she is silly*—when you told me to fix where my dress was torn?

QUENTIN: What about it?

MAGGIE: You wanted me to be . . . proud of myself. Didn't you?

QUENTIN, *surprised*: I guess I did, yes. . . . I did.

MAGGIE, *feeling she has budged him*: Would you like a drink?

QUENTIN, *relaxing*: I wouldn't mind. *Glancing around*: What's all the flowers?

MAGGIE, *pouring*: Oh, that's that dopey prince or a king or whatever he is. He keeps sending me a contract . . . whereas I get a hundred thousand dollars if we ever divorce. I'd be like a queen or something, but I only met him in El Morocco *once*! And I'm supposed to be his girl! *She laughs, handing him his drink.* I don't know why they print those things!

QUENTIN: Well, I guess everybody wants to touch you now.

MAGGIE: Cheers!

> *They drink; she makes a face.*

I hate the taste but I love the effect! Would you like to take off your shoes? I mean just to rest.

QUENTIN: I'm okay. I thought you sounded on the phone like something frightened you.

MAGGIE, *evasively*: No. I . . . You have to go home right away?

QUENTIN: You all alone here?

MAGGIE, *with a strong evasiveness*: I don't mind that, I've always been alone. Oh, hey!

> *As though afraid to lose his interest, she digs into a pile of papers beside the bed, coming up with a small framed photo.*

I cut your picture out of the paper last month. When you were defending that Reverend Harley Barnes in Washington? See? I framed it.

QUENTIN, *pleased and embarrassed*: What'd you do that for?

MAGGIE: It's funny how I found it. I was on the train . . .

QUENTIN: Is something frightening you, Maggie?

MAGGIE: No, don't worry! I'm just nervous you're here. See, what I did, they kept interviewing me and asking where you were born and all, and I didn't know what to answer. Whereas my father, see, he left when I was like eighteen months, and I just thought . . . if I could see him. And maybe he would like me. Or even not. Just so he'd look. I can't explain it.

QUENTIN: Maybe so you'd know who you were.

MAGGIE: Yes! So I took the train, he's got a business upstate there, and I called him from the station. And I said, "Can I see you?" And he said, "Who is it?" And I said, "It's Maggie, your daughter." Whereas he said I wasn't from him, although my mother always said I was. And he said, "I don't know who you are, see my lawyer." And I told him, "I just want you to look at me and—" And he hung up. *She laughs, lightly.* So I had time and I walked around the town and I thought maybe if I could find where he eats. And I would go in, and he'd see me and maybe . . . pick me up! *Laughs.* 'Cause my mother said he always liked beautiful girls!

QUENTIN: And then you'd tell him?

MAGGIE: I don't know. Maybe. Maybe . . . afterwards. I don't know why I tell you that . . . Oh, yes! On the train back I found this picture in the paper. And you see the way you're looking straight in the camera? That's very hard to do, you know . . . to look absolutely straight in?

QUENTIN: You mean I was looking at you.

MAGGIE: Yes! And I said, "I know who I am. I'm Quentin's friend." *Afraid she's gone too fast*: You want another drink or . . . I mean you don't have to do anything. You don't even have to see me again.

QUENTIN: Why do you say that?

MAGGIE: 'Cause I think it worries you.

QUENTIN: It does, yes.

MAGGIE: But why? I mean, can't you just be somebody's friend?

QUENTIN—*slight pause, and with resolve*: Yes. I can. It's that you're so beautiful, Maggie. I don't mean only your body and your face.

MAGGIE, *with a sudden rush of feeling*: I would do anything for you, Quentin. You—*It bursts from her*—you're like a god! S'use me I say that but I—

QUENTIN, *with half a laugh*: Maggie, anybody would have told you to mend your dress.

MAGGIE: No, they wouldn't.

QUENTIN: What then?

MAGGIE, *in great pain*: Laugh. Or just . . . try for a quick one. You know.

QUENTIN, *to Listener*: Yes! It's all so clear: the honor! The first honor . . . was that I hadn't tried to go to bed with her! God, the hypocrisy! . . . Because, I was only afraid, and she took it for a tribute to her . . . "value"! No wonder I can't find myself here!

> *He has gotten to his feet in agony.*

MAGGIE: Oh, hey—I christened a submarine! But you know what I did?

QUENTIN: What?

MAGGIE: I was voted the favorite of the Groton Shipyard! You know, by the workers. So the Admiral hand me the champagne bottle and I said, how come there's no workers in the ceremony, you know? And they all laughed! So I yelled down, and I got about ten of them to come up on the platform! Whereas they're the ones built it, right?

QUENTIN: That's wonderful!

MAGGIE: And you know what the Admiral said? I better watch out or I'll be a Communist. Honestly! So I said, "I don't know what's so terrible. . . . I mean they're for the poor people." Aren't they? The Communists?

QUENTIN: It's a lot more complicated, honey.

MAGGIE: But I mean, like when I was little I used to get free shoes from the Salvation Army. Although they never fit. *Embarrassed, with waning conviction*: But if the workers *do* everything why shouldn't they have the honor? Isn't that what you believe?

QUENTIN: I did, yes. But the question is whether the workers don't end up just where they are, and some new politicians on the stand.

MAGGIE: Oh. *With open longing and self-loss*: I wish I knew something!

QUENTIN: Honey, you know how to see it all with your own eyes; that's more important than all the books.

MAGGIE: But I don't know if it's true, what I see. But you do. You see and you know if it's true.

QUENTIN: What do you think I know?

MAGGIE, *some guard falling, her need rising*: Well like . . . that I was frightened.

QUENTIN: You frightened *now*? . . . You are, aren't you?

Maggie stares at him in tension; a long moment passes.

What is it, dear? You frightened to be alone here?

An involuntary half-sob escapes her. He sees she is in some great fear.

Why don't you call somebody to stay with you?

MAGGIE: I don't know anybody . . . like that.

QUENTIN—*slight pause*: Can I do anything? Don't be afraid to ask me.

MAGGIE—*in a struggle she finally says*: Would you . . . open that closet door?

QUENTIN—*he looks off, then back to her*: Just open it?

MAGGIE: Yes.

> *He walks into the dark periphery; she sits up warily, watching. He returns. And she lies back.*

QUENTIN: Do you . . . want to tell me something?

MAGGIE: I just never know what's right to say and I—

QUENTIN: Well, say it, and find out; what are people for? I'm not going to laugh. *Sits.* What is it?

MAGGIE, *with great difficulty*: When I start to go to sleep before. And suddenly I saw smoke coming out of that closet under the door. It started to fill the whole room! *She breaks off, near weeping.*

QUENTIN—*reaches and takes her hand*: Oh, kid, that's nothing to—

MAGGIE: But it kept coming and coming!

QUENTIN: But look—you've often dreamed such things, haven't you?

MAGGIE: But I was awake!

QUENTIN: Well, it was a waking dream. It just couldn't stay down till you went to sleep. These things can be explained if you trace them back.

MAGGIE: I know. I go to an analyst.

QUENTIN: Oh . . . then tell him about it, you'll figure it out.

MAGGIE: It's when I start to call you before.

> *She is now absorbed in her own connections.*

See, my mother . . . she used to get dressed in the closet. She was very . . . like moral, you know? But sometimes she'd smoke in there. And she'd come out—you know?—with a whole cloud of smoke around her.

QUENTIN: Well . . . possibly you felt she didn't want you to call me.

MAGGIE, *astounded*: How'd you know that?

QUENTIN: Because you said she was so moral. And here you're calling a married man.

MAGGIE: Yes! See, she tried to kill me once with a pillow on my face, whereas . . . I would turn out bad because of her . . . like her sin. And I have her hair, and the same back.

She turns half from him, showing a naked back.

'Cause I have a good back, see? Every masseur says.

QUENTIN: Yes, it is. It's beautiful. But it's no sin to call me.

MAGGIE, *shaking her head like a child—with a relieved laugh at herself*: Doesn't make me bad. Right?

QUENTIN: You're a very moral girl, Maggie.

MAGGIE, *delicately and afraid*: W—what's moral?

QUENTIN: You tell the truth, even against yourself. You're not pretending to be . . .

Turns out to the Listener, with a dread joy.

. . . innocent! Yes, that suddenly there was someone who—would not club you to death with their innocence! It's all laughable!

Felice begins to brighten, her arms raised, just as Mother appears and she is raising her arm . . .

MOTHER: I saw a star . . . .

MAGGIE: I bless you, Quentin!

Mother and Felice vanish as he turns back to Maggie, who takes up his photo.

Lot of nights when I go to sleep, I take your picture, and I bless you. You mind?

She has pressed the picture against her cheek. He bends to her, kisses her; for an instant she is unprepared, then starts to raise her arms to hold him. But he stands and backs away.

QUENTIN: I hope you sleep.

MAGGIE: I will now! *Lies back.* Honestly! I feel . . . all clear!

QUENTIN, *with a wave of his hand, backing away*: Good luck in London.

MAGGIE: And . . . what's moral, again?

QUENTIN: To live the truth.

MAGGIE: That's you!

QUENTIN: Not yet, dear; but I intend to try.

> *He halts. Across the room they look at one another. He walks back to her; now he bends in and she embraces him this time, offering herself, raising her body toward him. He stands, breaking it off. And as though he knows he is taking a step . . .*

Don't be afraid to call me if you need any help.

> *She is suddenly gone. Alone, he continues the thought.*

Any time . . .

> *Dan appears in crew-necked sweater with his book.*

. . . you need anything, you call, y'hear?

DAN: This family's behind you, Quentin.

> *Backing into darkness, with a wave of farewell.*

Any time you need anything . . .

> *Quentin, surprised, has turned quickly to Dan, who disappears.*

QUENTIN, *to the Listener, as he still stares at the empty space Dan has left*: You know? It isn't fraud, but some . . . disguise. I came to her like Dan . . . his goodness! No wonder I can't find myself!

> *Felice appears, about to remove the "bandage," and he grasps for the concept.*

. . . And that girl the other night.

> *Felice turns and goes.*

When she left. It's still not clear, but suddenly those two fixtures on my wall . . .

> *He walks toward a "wall," looking up.*

I didn't do it, but I wanted to. Like . . .

> *He turns and spreads his arms in crucifixion.*

. . . this!

> *In disgust he lowers his arms.*

. . . I don't know! Because she . . . *gave* me something! She . . . let me change her! As though I—*Cries out*—felt something! *He almost laughs.* What the hell am I trying to do, love *everybody*?

The line ends in self-contempt and anger. And suddenly, extremely fast, a woman appears in World War I costume—a Gibson Girl hat and veil over her face, ankle-length cloak, and in her hand a toy sailboat. She is bent over as though offering the boat to a little boy, and her voice is like a whisper, distant, obscure.

MOTHER: Quentin? Look what we brought you from Atlantic City—from the boardwalk!

The boy evidently runs away; Mother instantly is anxious and angering and rushes to a point and halts, as though calling through a closed door.

Don't lock this door! But darling, we didn't trick you, we took Dan because he's older and I wanted a rest! ... But Fanny told you we were coming back, didn't she? Why are you running that water? Quentin, stop that water! Ike, come quick! Break down the door! Break down the door!

She has rushed off into darkness, and Quentin has started after her as though to complete the memory. He halts, and speaks to the Listener.

QUENTIN: ... They sent me for a walk with the maid. When I came back the house was empty for a week. God, why is betrayal the only truth that sticks! ... Yes! *He almost laughs.* "Love everybody!" And I can't even mourn my own mother. It's monstrous.

The "park bench" lights. Maggie appears in a heavy white man's sweater, a red wig over a white angora skating cap, moccasins, and sun glasses.

MAGGIE, *to the empty bench*: Hi! It's me! *Lifting the glasses.* Maggie!

QUENTIN, *looking toward Maggie*: Or mourn her, either. Is it simply grief I want? ... No, this isn't mourning! ... Because there's too much hatred in it!

He has come away from the adoring Maggie to the chair, shaking his head.

... No, it's not that I think I killed her. It's—

An anonymous man passes Maggie, glances, and goes on out.

MAGGIE, *to the empty bench*: See? I told you nobody recognizes me! Like my wig?

QUENTIN: . . . that I can't find myself in it, it's like another man. Only the guilt comes. Yes, or the innocence!

MAGGIE, *sitting beside "him" on the bench*: When you go to Washington tonight . . . you know what I could do? I could get on a different car on the same train!

QUENTIN, *to Listener*: But is it enough to tell a man he is not-guilty? *Glances at her.* My name is on this man! Why can't I say "I"? *Turning toward her*: I did this. I want what I did! And I saw it once! I saw *Quentin* here! For one moment like the moon sees, I saw us both unblamed!

MAGGIE: Golly, I fell asleep the minute you left the other night! I didn't even hear you close the door! You like my wig? See? And moccasins!

Slight pause. Now he smiles.

QUENTIN: All you need is roller skates.

MAGGIE, *clapping her hands with joy*: You're funny!

QUENTIN, *half to Listener*: I keep forgetting . . . *Wholly to her*: . . . how beautiful you are. Your eyes make me shiver.

She is silent, adoring. He breaks it, sitting.

MAGGIE: Like to see my new apartment? There's no elevator even, or a doorman. Nobody would know. If you want to rest before you go to Washington.

He doesn't reply.

'Cause I just found out, I go to Paris after London. I'm on for two weeks, which is supposed to be unusual. But I won't be back for a while.

QUENTIN: How long will you be gone?

MAGGIE: About . . . six weeks, I think.

They both arrive at the same awareness: the separation is pain. Tears are in her eyes.

Quentin?

QUENTIN: Honey . . . *Takes her hand.* Don't look for anything more from me.

MAGGIE: I'm not! See, all I thought, if I went to Washington—

QUENTIN, *with a laugh*: What about London?

MAGGIE: Oh, they'll wait. 'Cause I could register in the hotel as Miss None.

QUENTIN: N-u-n?

MAGGIE: No—"n-o-n-e"—like nothing. I made it up once, 'cause I can never remember a fake name, so I just have to think of nothing and that's me! *She laughs with joy.* I've done it.

QUENTIN: It *is* a marvelous thought. The whole government's hating me, and meanwhile back at the hotel . . .

MAGGIE: That's what I mean! Just when that committee is knocking on your head you could think of me like naked. . . .

QUENTIN: What a lovely thought.

MAGGIE: And it would make you happy.

QUENTIN, *smiling warmly at her*: And nervous. But it is a lovely thought.

MAGGIE: Because it should all be one thing, you know? Helping people, and sex. You might even argue better the next day!

QUENTIN, *with a new awareness, astonishment*: You know?—There's one word written on your forehead.

MAGGIE: What?

QUENTIN: "Now."

MAGGIE: But what else is there?

QUENTIN: A future. And I've been carrying it around all my life, like a vase that must never be dropped. So you cannot ever touch anybody, you see?

MAGGIE: But why can't you just hold it in one hand?

    He laughs.

And touch with the other! I would never bother you, Quentin.

    He looks at his watch, as though beginning to calculate if there might not be time.

Can't somebody just give you something? Like when you're thirsty. And you drink, and walk away, that's all.

QUENTIN: But what about you?

MAGGIE: Well . . . I would have what I gave. *Slight pause.*

QUENTIN: You're all love, aren't you?

MAGGIE: That's all I am! A person could die any minute, you know. *Suddenly*: Oh, hey! I've got a will! *She digs into her pocket and brings out a folded sheet of notepaper.* Could . . . I show it to you?

QUENTIN, *taking it*: What do you want with a will?

MAGGIE: Well I'm going to do a lot of flying now and I just got my payment yesterday. Should I tell you how much?

QUENTIN: How much?

MAGGIE: Two hundred thousand dollars.

QUENTIN: Huh! You remember we sat right here, and I gave you five dollars?

MAGGIE, *with great love*: Yes!

> *They stare at each other.*

Really, Quentin, there's not even an elevator man.

QUENTIN: You want me to look at that? Honey, I've got to do one thing at a time. *He opens the will.*

MAGGIE: I understand!

> *He starts reading the will.*

See, I'm supposed to be like a millionaire in about two years!

> *Laughs; he goes on reading.*

Is it legal if it's not typewritten?

QUENTIN—*looks at her*: Who wrote this?

MAGGIE: My agency; mostly Andy. Whereas he had to leave for London this morning to set everything up. And it was in a big rush.

> *Not comprehending, he nods and reads on.*

But he's got a copy and I've got a copy.

> *He glances at her, bewildered.*

I mean, that's what he said; that we both have copies.

> *He turns the page, reads on.*

You got a haircut. I love the back of your head, it's sweet.

His brows knit now as he reads.

I'll shut up.

Finished reading, he stares ahead.

Or does it have to be typed?

QUENTIN: Who's this other signature?

MAGGIE: That's Jerry Moon. He's a friend of Andy in the building business, but he knows a lot about law so he signed it for a witness. I saw him sign it. In my bedroom. Isn't it good?

QUENTIN: It leaves everything to the agency.

MAGGIE: I know, but just for temporary, till I can think of somebody to put down.

QUENTIN: But what's all the rush?

MAGGIE: Well in case Andy's plane goes down. He's got five children, see, and his—

QUENTIN: But do you feel responsible for his family?

MAGGIE: Well, no. But he did help me, he loaned me money when I—

QUENTIN: A million dollars?

MAGGIE, *with a dawning awareness*: Well, not a million. *With fear*: You mean I shouldn't?

QUENTIN: Who's your lawyer?

Two boys with bats and gloves pass, see her, walk off backward, whispering.

MAGGIE: Well, nobody. Jerry has a lawyer and he checks. I mean what's good for Andy's good for me, right?

QUENTIN—*with a certain unwillingness, even a repugnance, about interfering, he sounds neutral*: Didn't anybody suggest you get your own lawyer?

MAGGIE, *with fading conviction*: But if you trust somebody, you trust them. . . . Don't you?

QUENTIN—*a decision seizes him; he takes her hand*: Come on, I'll walk you home.

MAGGIE, *standing*: Okay! 'Cause I mean if you trust somebody!

QUENTIN: I'm sorry, honey, I can't advise you. Maybe you get something out of this that I don't understand. Let's go.

MAGGIE: No, I'm not involved with Andy. I . . . don't really sleep around with everybody, Quentin.

QUENTIN: Come on.

MAGGIE, *suddenly brightening*: 'Cause . . . I was never a prostitute. I was with a lot of men, but I never got anything. Not even for a job. I mean I'm changing. My analyst says I used to think it was like charity—sex. Like I give to those in need? *Laughs shyly.* Whereas I'm not an institution! Will you come in for a minute, too?

QUENTIN, *taking her arm*: Sure.

> *A small gang of boys with baseball equipment obstructs them; one of the first pair points at her.*

FIRST BOY: It's Maggie, I told you!

MAGGIE, *pulling at Quentin's arm, defensively*: No, I just look like her, I'm Sarah None!

SECOND BOY: I can hear her voice!

QUENTIN: Let's go!

> *He tries to draw her off, but the boys grab her, and, strangely, she begins accepting pencils and pieces of paper to autograph.*

Hey!

CROWD: How about an autograph, Maggie?
>> Whyn't you come down to the club?
>> When's your next spectacular?
>> Hey, Mag, I got all your records!
>> Sing something!

> *Handing over a paper for her to sign.*

>> For my brother, Mag!
>> Take off your sweater, Mag, it's hot out!
>> How about that dance like you did on TV?

> *A boy wiggles sensually.*

> *Quentin has been thrust aside; he now reaches in, grabs her, and*

draws her away as she walks backward, still signing, laughing with them. The boys gone, she turns to him.

MAGGIE: I'm sorry!

QUENTIN: It's like they're eating you. You like that?

MAGGIE: No, but they're just people. Could you sit down till the train? All I got so far is this French Provincial. *Taking off her sweater*: You like it? I picked it out myself. And my bed, and my record player. But it could be a nice apartment, couldn't it?

In silence Quentin takes her hand; he draws her to him; he kisses her.

Enflamed:

I love you, Quentin. I would do anything for you. And I would never bother you, I swear.

QUENTIN: You're so beautiful it's hard to look at you.

MAGGIE: You didn't even see me! *Backing away.* Why don't you just stand there and I'll come out naked! Or isn't there a later train?

QUENTIN—*pause*: Sure. There's always a later train.

He starts unbuttoning his jacket.

MAGGIE: I'll put music!

QUENTIN—*now he laughs through his words*: Yeah, put music!

She rushes into the dark, and he strives for his moment. To the Listener as he opens his jacket:

Here, it was somewhere here! . . . I don't know, a . . . a fraud!

A driving jazz comes on and she comes back, still dressed.

MAGGIE: Here, let me take off your shoes!

She drops to his feet, starting to unlace. Stiffly, with a growing horror, he looks down at her. Now shapes move in the darkness. He moves his foot away involuntarily.

QUENTIN: Maggie?

MAGGIE, *looking up from the floor, leaving off unlacing*: Yes?

He looks around in the darkness, and suddenly his Father charges forward.

FATHER: What you *want*! Always what you *want*! Chrissake, *what are you?*

> *Now Louise appears, reading a book, but Dan is standing beside her, almost touching her with his hand.*

DAN: This family's behind you, kid.

> *And Mother, isolated, almost moving sensuously—and Quentin is moved, as though by them, away from Maggie.*

MOTHER: Oh, what poetry he brought me, Strauss, and novels and . . .

QUENTIN—*he roars out to all of them, his fists angrily in air against them*: But where is Quentin?

> *Going toward Mother in her longing.*

Yes, yes! But I know that treason! And the terror of complicity in that desire.

> *Turns toward Dan, who has moved alongside Father. The music breaks off.*

Yes, and to not be unworthy of those loyal, failing men! But where is Quentin? Instead of taking off my clothes, this—*He bends to Maggie, raises her to her feet*—posture!

MAGGIE: Okay. Maybe when I get back we—

QUENTIN: I have to say it to you, Maggie.

> *To Listener.*

Here it is, right here the killing fraud begins. *Pause.* You . . . have to tear up that will.

> *To Listener.*

Can't even go to bed without a principle! But how can you speak of love, she had been chewed and spat out by a long line of grinning men! Her name floating in the stench of locker rooms and parlor-car cigar smoke! She had the truth that day, I brought the lie that she had to be "saved"! From what—except my own contempt? . . . Heh?

> *He is evidently caught by the Listener's contradicting him, steps closer to the chair, avidly listening.*

MAGGIE, *to the empty space where Quentin was*: But I showed the will to my analyst, and he said it was okay. 'Cause a person like me has to have *somebody*.

QUENTIN: Maggie . . . honest men don't draw wills like that.

MAGGIE: But it's just for temporary. . . .

QUENTIN: Darling, if I went to Andy, and this adviser, and the analyst too, perhaps, I think they'd offer me a piece to shut up. They've got you on a table, honey, and they're carving you.

MAGGIE: But . . . I can't spend all that money anyway! I can't even *think* over twenty-five dollars!

QUENTIN: It's not the money they take, it's the dignity they destroy. You're not a piece of meat; you seem to think you owe people whatever they demand!

MAGGIE: I know. *She lowers her head with a cry, trembling with hope and shame.*

QUENTIN, *tilting up her face*: But Maggie, you're somebody! You're not a kid any more running around looking for a place to sleep! It's not only your success or that you're rich—you're straight, you're serious, you're first-class, people *mean* something to you; you don't have to go begging shady people for advice like some . . . some tramp.

> *With a sob of love and desperation, she slides to the floor and grasps his thighs, kissing his trousers. He watches, then suddenly lifts her and, with immense pity and joy:*

Maggie, stand up!

> *The music flies in now, and she smiles strangely through her tears, and with a kind of statement of her persisting nature begins unbuttoning her blouse, her body writhing to the beat within her clothing. And as soon as she starts her dance his head shakes . . . and to the Listener:*

No, not love; to stop impersonating, that's all! To live—*Groping*: —to live in good faith if only with my guts! To . . .

> *Suddenly Dan and Father appear together; and to them:*

Yes! To be "good" no more! Disguised no more! Afraid no more to show what Quentin, Quentin, Quentin . . . is!

Louise appears, talking.

LOUISE: You haven't even the decency to—

QUENTIN: That decency is murderous! Speak truth, not decency—
I curse the whole high administration of fake innocence! I declare
it, I am not innocent! Nor good!

> *A high tribunal dimly appears; a chairman bangs his gavel once;
> he is flanked by others looking down on Quentin from on high.
> Maggie is dropping her blouse.*

CHAIRMAN: But surely Reverend Barnes cannot object to answering whether he attended the Communist-run Peace Congress in
Prague, Czechoslovakia. No—no, counsel will not be allowed to
confer with the witness, this is not a trial! Any innocent man
would be . . .

QUENTIN: And this question—innocent! How many Negroes you
allow to vote in your patriotic district? And which of your social,
political, or racial sentiments would Hitler have disapproved? And
not a trial? You fraud, your "investigators" this moment are working this man's church to hound him out of it!

HARLEY BARNES—*appears rising to his feet; he has a clerical collar:*
I decline on the grounds of the First and Fifth Amendments to the
Constitution.

QUENTIN, *with intense sorrow:* But are we sure, Harley—I ask it,
I ask it—if the tables were turned, and they were in front of you—
would you permit *them* not to answer? Hateful men that they are?

> *Harley looks at him indignantly, suspiciously.*

I am not sure what we are upholding any more—are we good by
merely saying no to evil? Even in a righteous "no" there's some
disguise. Isn't it necessary . . . to say . . .

> *Harley is gone, and the tribunal. Maggie is there, snapping her
> fingers, letting down her hair.*

. . . to finally say yes . . . to *something?*

> *A smile of pain and longing has come onto his face, and Maggie
> expands now, slipping out of her skirt, dancing in place. He goes
> to her and grasps her body, moving with her serpentine motion.*

A fact . . . a fact . . . a thing.

> *Maggie embraces him and then lies down on the "bed" with the imagined Quentin.*

MAGGIE: Sing inside me.

> *Quentin moves to the chair facing the Listener; she continues on the bed behind him as he sits.*

QUENTIN: Even condemned, unspeakable like all truth!

MAGGIE: Become happy.

QUENTIN, *still to Listener*: Contemptible like all truth.

MAGGIE: That's all I am.

QUENTIN: Covered like truth with slime; blind, ignorant.

MAGGIE: But nobody ever said to me, stand up!

QUENTIN: The blood's fact, the world's blind gut . . . yes!

MAGGIE: Now.

QUENTIN: To this, yes.

MAGGIE: Now . . . now.

> *Her recorded number ends and only the thumping needle in the empty groove is heard through the lengthening darkness. Then her voice, pillowed and soft.*

MAGGIE: Quentin?

> *Light finds her prone on a bed, alone on the stage, a sheet partly covering her naked body. Her chin rests languidly on her hands. She glances toward a point, off.*

Quenny? That soap is odorless, so you don't have to worry.

> *Slight pause.*

It's okay! Don't rush; I love to wait for you!

> *Her eye falls on his shoe on the floor. She picks it up, strokes it.*

I love your shoes. You have good taste!

> *Slight pause.*

S'use me I didn't have anything for you to eat, but I didn't know! I'll get eggs, though, case maybe in the mornings. And steaks—

case at night. I mean just in case. You could have it just the way you want, just any time.

>*Quentin stands looking front; she speaks to empty space from the bed.*

Like me?

>*He glances back at her adoring face, as Holga appears above in the airport, looking about for him. Maggie remains on the bed, stroking his shoe.*

QUENTIN, *glancing at Maggie*: It's all true, but it isn't the truth. I know it because it all comes back too cheap; my bitterness is making me lie. I'm afraid. To make a promise. Because I don't know who'll be making it. I'm a stranger to my life.

MAGGIE—*she has lifted a tie off the floor*: Oh, your tie got all wrinkled! I'm sorry! But hey, I have a tie! *Jumping up with the sheet around her.* It's beautiful, a regular man's tie—*Catching herself*: I . . . just happen to have it!

>*She tries to laugh it off and goes into darkness. Holga is gone.*

QUENTIN: I tell you, below this fog of tawdriness and vanity, there is a law in this disaster, and I saw it once as hard and clear as a statute. But I think I saw it . . . with some love. Or simply wonder, but not blame. It's . . . like my mother; so many of my thoughts of her degenerate into some crime; the truth is she was a light to me whenever it was dark. I loved that nut, and only love does make her real and mine. Or can one ever remember love? It's like trying to summon up the smell of roses in a cellar. You might see a rose, but never the perfume. And that's the truth of roses, isn't it—the perfume?

>*Maggie appears in light in a wedding dress; Carrie, the maid, is just placing a veiled hat on her head; Lucas, the designer, is on his knees hurriedly fixing the last hem. Maggie is turning herself wide-eyed in a mirror. Quentin begins to rise.*

MAGGIE: Okay! Let him in, Carrie! Thanks, Lucas, but I don't want him to wait any more, the ceremony is for three! Hurry, please!

>*Lucas sews faster; Carrie goes to a point, calls down.*

CARRIE: Mister Quentin? You can see her now.

QUENTIN: I want to see her with . . . that love again! Why is it so hard? Standing there, that wishing girl, that victory in lace. We had turned all mockery to purpose, and purpose moved around us like the natural shadows of the day!

MAGGIE, *looking ahead on the edge of life as Lucas bites off the last threads*: You won't hardly know me any more, Lucas! He saved me, I mean it! I've got a new will and I even changed my analyst, I've got a wonderful doctor now! And we're going to do all my contracts over, which I never got properly paid. And Ludwig Reiner's taking me! And he won't take even opera singers unless they're, you know, like artists! No matter how much you want to pay him. I didn't even dare but Quentin made me go—and now he took me, imagine! Ludwig Reiner!

> *She turns, seeing Quentin entering. An awe of the moment takes them both; Lucas goes. Carrie lightly touches Maggie's forehead and silently prays, and walks off.*

QUENTIN: Oh, my darling. How perfect you are.

MAGGIE: Like me?

QUENTIN: Good God—to come home every night—to *you*!

> *He starts for her open-armed, laughing, but she touches his chest, excited and strangely fearful.*

MAGGIE: You still don't have to do it, Quentin. I could just come to you whenever you want.

QUENTIN—*it hurts him but he tries to laugh again*: You just can't believe in something good really happening. But it's real, darling, you're my wife!

MAGGIE, *with a hush of fear on her voice*: I want to tell you something.

QUENTIN: I know enough. Come.

MAGGIE, *slipping her hand out of his*: I just want to tell you!

QUENTIN: Darling, you're always making new revelations, but that stuff doesn't matter any more.

MAGGIE, *pleased, and like a child wanting some final embrace*: But the reason I went into analysis! I never told you *that*!

QUENTIN, *smiling above his own foreboding*: All right, what?

MAGGIE: 'Cause you said we have to love what happened, didn't you? Even the bad things?

QUENTIN, *seriously now, to match her intensity*: Yes, I did.

MAGGIE: I . . . was with two men . . . the same day. *She has turned her eyes from him.* I mean the same day, see. But I didn't realize it till that night. And I got very scared. *She almost weeps now, and looks at him, subservient and oddly chastened.* I'll always love you, Quentin. But don't be afraid what people say, we could just tell them we changed our mind, and get in the car and maybe go to a motel. . . .

> *Anonymous men appear in the farthest distance and vanish as Quentin shakes his head.*

QUENTIN: Look, darling. It wasn't you. . . . *Reaching for her hand again*: Come now.

MAGGIE: But maybe in a way it was. In a way! I don't know!

QUENTIN: Sweetheart, everyone does things that . . .

> *To Listener, with sudden realization:*

Here, here is part of it! One part is that . . .

> *Back to her:*

An event itself, dear, is not important; it's what you took from it. Whatever happened to you, this is what you made of it and I love this.

> *To Listener, rapidly:*

. . . Yes! That we conspired to violate the past, and the past is holy and its horrors are holiest of all!

> *Turning back to Maggie:*

And . . . something . . . more . . .

MAGGIE, *with hope now*: Maybe . . . it would even make me a better wife, right?

QUENTIN, *with hope against the pain*: That's the way to talk!

MAGGIE, *with gladness, seeing a fruit of the horror*: 'Cause I'm not curious! You be surprised, a lot of women, they smile and their husbands never know, but they're curious. But I *know*—I have a king, and *I know*!

> *A wedding march strikes up. It shatters her fragile vision; he takes her arm.*

There's people who . . . going to laugh at you.

QUENTIN: Not any more, dear, they're going to see what I see. Come!

MAGGIE, *not moving with him*: What do you see? Tell me! *Bursting out of her*: 'Cause I think . . . you were ashamed once, weren't you?

QUENTIN: I see your suffering, Maggie; and once I saw it, all shame fell away.

MAGGIE: You . . . were ashamed!?

QUENTIN, *with difficulty*: Yes. But you're a victory, Maggie, for yourself and me. And somehow for everyone. *He kisses her hand.* Believe it, darling, you're like a flag to me, a kind of proof, somehow, that people can win.

MAGGIE: And you . . . you won't ever look at any other woman, right?

QUENTIN: Darling, a wife can be loved! You never saw it but . . .

MAGGIE, *with a new intensity of conflict*: Before, though—why did you kiss that Elsie?

QUENTIN: Just hello. She always throws her arms around people.

MAGGIE: But . . . why'd you let her rub her body against you?

QUENTIN—*laughs*: She wasn't rubbing her . . .

MAGGIE, *downing a much greater anxiety*: I saw it. And you stood there.

QUENTIN, *trying to laugh*: Maggie, it was a meaningless gesture.

MAGGIE: But you told me yourself that I have to look for the meaning of things, didn't you? You want me to be like I used to be? Like nothing means anything, it's all a fog? *Now pleadingly, and vaguely wronged*: I'm just trying to understand; you mustn't laugh. Why did you let her do that?

QUENTIN: She came up to me and threw her arms around me, what could I do?

MAGGIE—*a flash of contemptuous anger*: What do you mean? You just tell her to knock it off!

QUENTIN, *taken aback*: I . . . don't think you want to sound like this, honey.

MAGGIE, *frightened she has shown a forbidden side*: Sound like what?

QUENTIN, *trying to brush it away*: Darling, you're just frightened and it magnifies every threat. Come, they're waiting.

> *He puts her arm in his; they turn to go.*

MAGGIE, *almost in tears*: Teach me, Quentin! I don't know how to be!

QUENTIN: Yes, darling. Now we start to be. Both of us.

> *They begin moving in processional manner toward a group of guests.*

MAGGIE: It's that nobody's here . . . from me. I'm like a stranger here! If my mother or my father or anybody who loved me—

QUENTIN: Be calm, dear, everyone here adores you.

> *Now as Maggie speaks she continues in processional tread, but he remains behind, staring at her; and she goes on with "him," her arm still held as before, but in midair now.*

MAGGIE: I'm sorry if I sounded that way, but you want me to say what I feel, don't you? See, till you, I never said anything, Quentin; you like gave me my feelings to say! You don't want me just smiling, like most women, do you?

> *During her speech Louise has appeared.*

QUENTIN, *as against the vision of Louise*: No. *Say* what you feel; the truth is on our side; always say it!

> *Louise is gone.*

MAGGIE, *faltering, but going on*: You're not holding me!

QUENTIN, *half the stage away now, and turning toward the empty air*: I am, darling, I'm with you!

MAGGIE, *as she walks into darkness*: I'm going to be a good wife, I'm going to be a good wife.... Quentin, I don't feel it!

QUENTIN, *both frustrated and with an appeal to her*: I'm holding you! See everybody smiling, adoring you? Look at the orchestra guys making a V for victory! Everyone loves you, darling! Why are you sad?

> *Suddenly, the Wedding March is gone as from the far depths of the stage, her shape undefined, she calls out with a laugh.*

MAGGIE: Surprise! You like it? They rushed it while we were away!

QUENTIN—*a slight pause; they are half a stage apart*: Yes, it's beautiful!

> *The dialogue is now condensed, like time swiftly passing in the mind.*

MAGGIE: See how large it makes the living room? And I want to take down that other wall too! Okay?

QUENTIN, *not facing her direction; to his memory of it*: But we just finished putting those walls in.

MAGGIE: Well it's only money; I want it big, like a castle for you! You want it beautiful, don't you?

QUENTIN: It's lovely, dear, but ... maybe wait till next year with the other wall. We're behind in the taxes, darling.

MAGGIE: But we could die tomorrow! Used to say, I have one word written on my forehead—why can't it be beautiful now? I get all that money next year.

QUENTIN: But see, dear, you owe almost all of it....

MAGGIE: Quentin, don't hold the future like a vase—touch now, touch me! I'm here, and it's now!

QUENTIN: Okay! Tear it down! Make it beautiful! Do it now! Maybe I *am* too cautious. Forgive me.

> *Her voice is suddenly heard in a vocal number. He breaks into a genuine smile of joy.*

Maggie, sweetheart—that's magnificent!

Now she appears, in blouse, leotards, high heels, listening and pacing. Several executives in dark suits appear, listening carefully.

MAGGIE: No! Tell me the truth! That piano's off, you're not listening!

QUENTIN: But nobody'll ever notice that.

A pianist moves near her out of the executive group.

MAGGIE: I know the difference! Don't you want me to be good? I *told* Weinstein I wanted Johnny Block but they give me this fag and he holds back my beat! Nobody listens to me, I'm a joke!

QUENTIN: All right, dear, maybe if I talked to Weinstein—

MAGGIE: No, don't get mixed up in my crummy business, you've got an important case . . .

QUENTIN—*he moves to a point and demands*: Weinstein, get her Johnny Block!

The music turns over into another number and her voice, swift, sure.

There now! Listen now!

She listens in suspense; he almost struts with his power.

See? There's no reason to get upset, just tell me and I'll talk to these people any time you—

MAGGIE: Oh, thank you, darling! See? They respect you. Ask Ludwig, soon as you come in the studio my voice flies! Oh, I'm going to be a good wife, Quentin, I just get nervous sometimes that I'm—*She sits as the music goes out*—only bringing you my problems. But I want my stuff to be perfect, and all they care is if they can get rich on it.

The executives are gone.

QUENTIN: Exactly, dear—so how can you look to them for your self-respect? Come, why don't we go out for a walk? We never walk any more. *He sits on his heels beside her.*

MAGGIE: You love me?

QUENTIN: I adore you. I just wish you could find some joy in your life.

MAGGIE: Quentin, I'm a joke that brings in money.

QUENTIN: I think it's starting to change, though—you've got a great band now, and Johnny Block, and the best sound crew. . . .

MAGGIE: Only because I fought for it. You'd think somebody'd come to me and say, Look, Maggie, you made us all this money, now we want you to develop yourself, what can we do for you?

QUENTIN: Darling, they'd be selling frankfurters if there were more money in it, how can you look to them for love?

MAGGIE, *alone, alone*: But where will I look?

QUENTIN, *thrown down*: Maggie, how can you say that?

MAGGIE—*she stands; there is an underlying suspiciousness now*: When I walked into the party you didn't even put your arms around me. I felt like one of those *wives* or something!

QUENTIN: Well, Donaldson was in the middle of a sentence and I—

MAGGIE: So what? *I walked into the room!* I hire him, he doesn't hire me!

QUENTIN: But he is directing your TV show and I was being polite to him.

MAGGIE: You don't have to be ashamed of me, Quentin. I had a right to tell him to stop those faggy jokes at my rehearsal. Just because he's cultured? I'm the one the public pays for, not Donaldson! Ask Ludwig Reiner what my value is!

QUENTIN: I married you, Maggie, I don't need Ludwig's lecture on your value.

MAGGIE, *looking at him with strange eyes—with a strange laugh*: Why . . . why you so cold?

QUENTIN: I'm not cold, I'm trying to explain what happened.

MAGGIE: Well, take me in your arms, don't explain.

He takes her in his arms, kisses her, and she plaintively instructs: Not like that. *Hold* me.

QUENTIN—*he tries to hold her tighter, then releases her*: Let's go for a walk, honey. Come on . . .

MAGGIE, *sinking*: What's the matter?

Louise appears, playing solitaire.

QUENTIN: Nothing.

MAGGIE: But Quentin . . . you should look at me more. I mean . . . like I *existed* or something. Like you used to look—out of your *self*.

Louise vanishes. Maggie moves away into darkness, deeply discouraged.

QUENTIN, *alone*: I adore you, Maggie; I'm sorry; it won't ever happen again. Never! You need more love than I thought. But I've got it, and I'll make you see it, and when you do you're going to astound the world!

A rose light floods a screen; Maggie emerges in a dressing gown, indicating an unseen window.

MAGGIE: Surprise! You like it? See the material?

QUENTIN: Oh, that's lovely! How'd you think of that?

MAGGIE: All you gotta do is close them and the sun makes the bed all rose.

QUENTIN, *striving for joy*: Yes, it's beautiful! You see? An argument doesn't mean disaster! Oh, Maggie, I never knew what love was! *Takes her in his arms.*

MAGGIE, *her spirit gradually falling*: Case during the day, like maybe you get the idea to come home and we make love again in daytime. *She ends sitting in a weakness; nostalgically*: Like last year, remember? In the winter afternoons? And once there was still snow on your hair. See, that's all I am, Quentin.

QUENTIN: I'll come home tomorrow afternoon.

MAGGIE: Well don't *plan* it.

He laughs, but she looks at him; her stare is piercing. His laugh dies.

QUENTIN: What is it? See, I don't want to hide things any more, darling. The truth saves, always remember that—tell me, what's bothering you?

MAGGIE, *shaking her head, seeing*: I'm not a good wife. I take up so much of your work.

QUENTIN: No, dear. I only said that because you—*Striving, against his true resentment*—you kind of implied that I didn't fight the network hard enough on that penalty, and I got it down to twenty thousand dollars. They had a right to a hundred when you didn't perform.

MAGGIE, *with rising indignation*: But can't I be sick? I was sick!

QUENTIN: I know, dear, but the doctor wouldn't sign the affidavit.

MAGGIE, *furious at him*: I had a pain in my side, for Christ's sake, I couldn't stand straight! You don't believe me, do you!

QUENTIN: Maggie, I'm only telling you the legal situation.

MAGGIE: Ask Ludwig what you should do! You should've gone in there roaring! 'Stead of a polite liberal and affidavits and—

QUENTIN, *hurt*: Don't say that, Maggie.

MAGGIE: Well, ask him! You don't know what a star's rights are! I make millions for those people!

QUENTIN: Maggie, I always thought I was a pretty good lawyer. . . .

MAGGIE: I'm not saying Ludwig is a lawyer.

QUENTIN: I know, dear, but he's always got these brave solutions but the two-three times I've tried to pin him down to specifics he gets full of oxygen.

MAGGIE: Now you're hurt! I can't *say* anything!

QUENTIN: Well, honey, I'm putting in forty per cent of my time on your problems.

MAGGIE: You are not putting—

QUENTIN, *horrified she doesn't know—an outburst*: Maggie, I keep a log; I know what I spend my time on!

> *She looks at him shaking her head; mortally wounded, tears in her eyes. She goes to a bottle and pours.*

I'm sorry, darling, but when you talk like that I feel a little . . . like a fool. Don't start drinking; please.

She drinks.

Look, I don't object to the time I spend, I'm happy to do it, but—

MAGGIE: Should never gotten married. I knew it. Soon's they got married it all changes. Every man I ever knew they hate their wives.

QUENTIN: Honey, it always comes down to the same thing, don't you see? Now listen to me. *Turns her.* You're still proceeding on the basis that you're alone. That you can be disposed of. And the slightest contradiction of your wishes makes the earth tremble. But—

MAGGIE: You taught me speak out, Quentin, and when I do you get mad.

QUENTIN: I'm not mad, I'm frustrated that you can't seem to pick up the joy we could have. My greatest happiness is when I know I've helped to make you smile, to make you—

MAGGIE: But the only reason I went to Ludwig was so you'd be proud of me, so you could say, "See? I found her she was a little lost nut, and look, look what became of Maggie!" It's all for you, that's why I want it good!

QUENTIN: Then what are we arguing about? We want the same thing, you see?

Suddenly to Listener:

Power! Yes, the power, the power to . . . to . . . Wait a minute, I had it, and I lost it.

MAGGIE, *pouring another drink*: So maybe the best thing is if I get a lawyer . . . you know, just a stranger.

QUENTIN—*slight pause; hurt*: Okay.

MAGGIE: It's nothing against you; but see, like that girl in the orchestra, that cellist—I mean, Andy took too much but he'd have gone in there and got rid of her. I mean, you don't laugh when a singer goes off key.

QUENTIN: But she said she coughed.

MAGGIE, *furiously*: She didn't cough, she laughed! And you stand there going ho-ho-ho to her high-class jokes! Christ sake, just because she played in a symphony?

QUENTIN: Maggie, I stopped by to pick you up, I said hello to her and—

MAGGIE: I'm not finishing this tape if she's in that band tomorrow! I'm entitled to my conditions, Quentin! *Commanding*: And I don't have to plead with anybody! I want her out!

QUENTIN, *quietly*: All right. I'll call Weinstein in the morning.

MAGGIE: You won't. You're too polite.

QUENTIN: I've done it before, Maggie; three others in three different bands.

MAGGIE: Well, so what? You're my husband. You're supposed to do that. Aren't you?

QUENTIN: But I can't pretend to enjoy demanding people be fired.

MAGGIE: But if it was your daughter you'd get angry, wouldn't you? Instead of apologizing for her?

QUENTIN—*envisions it*: I guess I would, yes. I'm sorry. I'll do it in the morning.

MAGGIE, *with desperate warmth*: That's all I mean. If I want something you should ask yourself why, why does she want it, not why she shouldn't have it. That's why I don't smile, I feel I'm fighting all the time to make you *see*. You're like a little boy, you don't see the knives people hide.

QUENTIN: I see the knives, but . . . It's the same thing again. You still don't believe you're not alone.

MAGGIE: Then make me believe it!

QUENTIN: I'm trying, darling, but sometimes you say a thing that cuts me down like a . . . Maggie, I'm not cold to you.

MAGGIE: I didn't mean you're cold. It's just . . . I've seen such terrible things, Quentin. I never told you most of it. And when you're alone all you have is what you can see. Ask my doctor—I see more than most people, 'cause I had to protect myself.

QUENTIN: But sweetheart, that's all gone. You've got a husband now who loves you.

Pause. She seems to fear greatly.

MAGGIE: But it's not all gone. When your mother tells me I'm getting fat, I know where I am—and when you don't do anything about it.

QUENTIN: But what can I do?

MAGGIE: Slap her down, that's what you do!

QUENTIN: But she says anything comes into her head, dear.

MAGGIE: She insulted me! She's jealous of me!

QUENTIN: Maggie, she adores you.

MAGGIE: What are you trying to make me think, I'm crazy?

QUENTIN: Why does everything come down to—

MAGGIE: I'm not crazy!

QUENTIN, *carefully, on eggs*: The thought never entered my mind, darling. I'll . . . talk to her.

MAGGIE, *mimicking him as though he were weak*: "I'll talk to her." She hates me!

QUENTIN: I'll tell her to apologize.

MAGGIE: But at least get a little angry!

QUENTIN: All right, I'll do it.

> *She drinks.*

MAGGIE: I'm not going to work tomorrow.

> *She lies down on the "bed" as though crushed.*

QUENTIN: Okay.

MAGGIE, *half springing up*: You know it's not "okay"! You're scared to death they'll sue me, why don't you say it?

QUENTIN: I'm not scared to death; it's just that you're so wonderful in this show and it's a pity to—

MAGGIE, *sitting up furiously*: All you care about is money! Don't shit me!

> *The anonymous men appear in the distance.*

QUENTIN, *quelling a fury—his voice very level*: Maggie, don't use that language with me, will you?

MAGGIE: Calling me vulgar, that I talk like a truck driver! Well, that's where I come from. I'm for Negroes and Puerto Ricans and truck drivers!

QUENTIN: Then why do you fire people so easily?

MAGGIE—*her eyes narrowing, she is seeing him anew*: Look. You don't want me. What the hell are you doing here?

QUENTIN, *with a quavering, mountainous restraint*: I live here. And you do too, but you don't know it yet. But you're going to. I . . .

Father appears.

FATHER: Where's he going, I need him! What are you?

And he is gone.

QUENTIN: I'm here, and I stick it. And one day you're going to catch on. Now go to sleep, I'll be back in ten minutes, I'd like to take a walk.

He starts out and she comes to attention.

MAGGIE: Where you going to walk?

QUENTIN: Just around the block.

She watches him carefully. He sees her suspicion.

There's nobody else, kid; I just want to walk.

MAGGIE, *with great suspicion*: 'Kay.

He goes a few yards, halts, turns to see her taking a pill bottle and unscrewing the top.

QUENTIN, *coming back*: You can't take pills on top of whisky, dear.

He has reached for them; she pulls them away but he grabs them again and puts them in his pocket.

That's how it happened the last time. And it's not going to happen again. Never. I'll be right back.

MAGGIE—*she pours again*: Why you wear those pants?

He turns back to her, knowing what is coming.

I told you the seat is too tight.

QUENTIN: Well, they made them too tight, but I can take a walk in them.

MAGGIE: Fags wear pants like that; I told you.

She drinks again. It is so pathological he looks with amazed eyes.

They attract each other with their asses.

QUENTIN: You calling me a fag now?

MAGGIE—*she is very drunk*: Just I've known fags and some of them didn't even know themselves that they were. And I didn't know if you knew about that.

QUENTIN: That's a hell of a way to reassure yourself, Maggie.

MAGGIE, *staggering slightly*: I'm allowed to say what I see . . .

QUENTIN: You trying to get me to throw you out? Is that what it is? So it'll get real?

MAGGIE, *pointing at him, at his control*: Wha's that suppose to be, strong and silent? I mean what is it?

She stumbles and falls. He makes no move to pick her up.

QUENTIN, *standing over her, quite knowing she is beyond understanding*: And now I walk out, huh? And it's real again, huh?

He picks her up angrily.

Is that what you want?

MAGGIE, *breaking from him*: I mean what *is it*?

She pitches forward; he catches her and roughly puts her on the bed.

Wha's the angle? I mean what is it?

She gets on her feet again.

You gonna wait till I'm old? You know what another cab driver said to me today? "I'll give you fifty dollars."

An open sob, wild and contradictory, flies out of her.

You know what's fifty dollars to a cab driver?

Her pain moves into him, his anger is swamped with it.

Go ahead, you can go; I can even walk a straight line, see? Look, see?

She walks with arms out, one foot in front of the other.

So what is it, heh? I mean what is it? I mean you want dancing? You want dancing?

QUENTIN: Please don't do that.

Breathlessly she turns on the phonograph and goes into a hip-flinging, broken ankle step around him.

MAGGIE: I mean what do you want! What is it?

He hasn't been looking at her, but beyond her, and now she starts tumbling about and he catches her and lays her down on the bed.

I mean, you gonna wait till I'm old? Or what? I mean what is it?

She lies there gasping. He stares down at her, addressing the Listener.

QUENTIN: That there is a love; limitless; a love not even of persons but blind, blind to insult, blind to the spear in the flesh, like justice blind, like . . .

Felice appears. Quentin slowly raises up his arms; holds them there. But his face is drawn together in his quest. Maggie speaks from the bed, half-asleep.

MAGGIE: Hey? Why?

Felice vanishes. He lowers his arms, peering for his answer, as . . .

I mean what do you want? Whyn't you beat it? I mean what is it?

Father appears.

FATHER: What are . . .

Quentin shakes his head, an unformed word of negation in his mouth.

Dan appears.

DAN: This family is always behind you, boy; anything you need, just . . .

Mickey appears; Quentin moves toward him.

MICKEY: . . . That we both go back, Lou, you and I together; and name the names.

QUENTIN, *shaking the vision out of his head as false and crying out—as Dan and Father disappear*: No! I had it! In whose name you turn your back! I saw it clear! I saw the name!

Lou appears on high; the approaching sound of a subway train is heard and he seems to fall off a platform to the wracking squeal of brakes, crying.

LOU: Quentin!

He is gone, and Mickey is gone. Quentin's hands are a vise against his head. The tower lights as . . .

QUENTIN, *on new level of angry terror*: In whose name? In whose blood-covered name do you look into a face you loved, and say, Now, you have been found wanting, and now in your extremity you die! It had a name, it . . .

Behind his back, in the farthest extremity of the stage, hardly visible excepting as a bent-over shape, Mother appears in pre-World War I costume, calling in a strange whisper:

MOTHER: Quentin? Quentin?

She is moving rapidly through shadow. He hurries toward her, but in fear.

QUENTIN: Hah? Hah?

MOTHER: See what we brought you from Atlantic City! From the boardwalk!

A tremendous crash of surf spins him about, and Mother is gone and the light of the moon is rising on the pier.

QUENTIN: . . . By the ocean. That cottage. That last night.

Maggie in a rumpled wrapper, a bottle in her hand, her hair in snags over her face, staggers out to the edge of the "pier" and stands in the sound of the surf. Now she starts to topple over the edge of the "pier" and he rushes to her and holds her in his hands. She slowly turns around and sees it's he. Now the sound of jazz from within is heard, softly.

MAGGIE: You were loved, Quentin; no man was ever loved like you.

QUENTIN, *releasing her*: Carrie tell you I called? My plane couldn't take off all day. . . .

MAGGIE, *drunk, but aware*: I was going to kill myself just now. *She walks past him. He is silent. She turns.* Or don't you believe that either?

QUENTIN, *with an absolute calm, a distance, but without hostility*: I saved you twice, why shouldn't I believe it? *Going toward her*: This dampness is bad for your throat, you oughtn't be out here.

MAGGIE—*she defiantly sits, her legs dangling*: Where've *you* been?

QUENTIN: I've been in Chicago. I told you. The Hathaway estate.

MAGGIE—*a sneer*: Estates!

QUENTIN: Well, I have to make a living before I save the world.

He goes into the bedroom, removing his jacket.

MAGGIE, *from the pier*: Didn't you hear what I told you?

QUENTIN: I heard it. I'm not coming out there, Maggie, it's too wet.

She looks out a moment, wide-eyed at the neutrality of his tone; then gets up and unsteadily comes into the room. He is taking off his tie.

MAGGIE: What's *this* all about?

QUENTIN: Just going to sleep. I'm very tired. I don't feel too hot.

MAGGIE: Tired.

QUENTIN: Yep. I can get tired too.

MAGGIE: Poor man.

QUENTIN: Not any more, no.

He sits on the bed unlacing his shoes. Sensing, she sits on a chair, the pill bottle in her hand.

MAGGIE, *like a challenge to him*: I didn't go to rehearsal today.

QUENTIN: I didn't think you did.

MAGGIE: I called Weinstein; I'm not working on his label any more and I don't care if he's got ten contracts. And I called the network; I'm not doing that stupid show, and I don't owe it to them regardless of any promise you made me make. I'm an artist and I don't have to do stupid shows no matter what contract!

QUENTIN: Maggie, I'm not your lawyer any more; tell it to—

MAGGIE: I told him. And he's getting me out of both contracts. And no arguments either.

QUENTIN: Good. I'll sleep in the living room. I've got to rest.

He starts out.

MAGGIE, *holding up the bottle*: Here, count them if you want to, I only took a few.

QUENTIN: I'm not counting pills any more, Maggie, I've given up being the policeman. But if you want to, I wish you'd tell me how many you had before I came. 'Cause they should know that in case they have to pump you out tonight.

MAGGIE, *hurt and bewildered*: What is this?

QUENTIN: Just that I can't pull on the other end of that rope any more. And I see the signs, honey, so I'm telling you in advance. The last two times when we got you out of it you thanked me for saving your life, and for days everything was warm and sweet. I'm not your analyst, but if this is how you create a happy reunion, forget it—this time I call the ambulance, so if you do wake up it'll be in the hospital, and that means the newspapers. I'm just trying to remove one of the motives, if a happy reunion is one of them— because I'm not going to be the rescuer any more. It's only fair to tell you, I just haven't got it any more. They're your pills and your life; you keep the count.

He starts out.

MAGGIE: What. . . . what's all this? Well, don't run away like a kid. What is all this?

QUENTIN—*halts; a pause*: Well . . . one thing is that I've been fired. And that's what I've been doing in Chicago. Max is there and I went to convince him that I oughtn't be let out of the firm.

MAGGIE: You're not fired.

QUENTIN: In fact, it's the second time in six months. I can't make a decision any more without something sits up inside me and busts out laughing.

MAGGIE: That my fault, heh?

QUENTIN: Maggie, I only tell it to you so you'll understand that the question is no longer whether you'll survive, but also whether I will. Because I'm backed up to the edge of the cliff, and I haven't one inch left behind me. And that's the difference tonight, Maggie.

So take care what you ask me, dear, because all I've got left is the truth. You know that feeling?

> *They hold each other's gaze. She unscrews the bottle and takes out a pill and swallows it.*

Okay.

> *He sits on the bed, and puts his shoes on again.*

MAGGIE: What are you doing?

QUENTIN: I'll sleep at the inn tonight. I think you're safer without me here. I think I've turned into some kind of ogre to you; and I haven't the strength to try to correct it any more.

> *He gets his tie.*

MAGGIE—*her speech thicker, but she is doped rather than drunk*: Don't . . . do that.

> *He looks at her lost face.*

Please. Please . . . sit down.

> *And as she did when they first met, but in a caricature of that invitingness, she indicates a chair.*

Could you . . . just while I . . . go to sleep? Please?

QUENTIN, *gently moved*: Okay, if you lie down and go to sleep.

MAGGIE: I'll . . . lie down here. See?

> *She quickly goes to the bed, clutching her pills, and lies down.*

See?

> *He sits facing her, a yard away. Silence.*

'Member? How used talk to me till I fell asleep?

QUENTIN: I've sat beside you for days and weeks at a time, Maggie, but you never remember. I've taken you for long drives to soothe you; sailed you around the bay for hours and my office looking high and low for me, but all you remember is the bad.

MAGGIE: Could you stay . . . like five minutes?

QUENTIN—*pause; he tries not to weep*: Yes.

MAGGIE—*slight pause; suddenly she puts the pills on the floor*: See? I'm not taking any more.

> *He is silent.*

I only had . . . about fifteen, I think. You . . . you can have the bottle if you want, even.

QUENTIN, *without rancor; explaining*: I don't want the bottle; I'm not the policeman any more.

MAGGIE: Please don't call the ambulance.

QUENTIN: Then don't take any more. I just can't go through it alone again, and I'm telling you.

MAGGIE—*slight pause*: You going back to your former wife, right?

QUENTIN: No, I've . . . *been* there.

MAGGIE: What then?

QUENTIN—*long pause*: Well, the first thing I've got to do is . . . get somebody to take care of you.

MAGGIE, *very carefully*: What do you mean, take care of me?

QUENTIN—*pause; under terrific stress he begins to touch his face, then puts his hand down*: I talked to your doctor this afternoon.

MAGGIE—*the terror growing*: About what? Thought you said your plane didn't take off.

QUENTIN: I was lying again, but there's no point to it any more. I just didn't want to have this conversation when you—

MAGGIE: I hear everything; what'd you talk to my doctor about? You going to put me somewhere? Is that it?

QUENTIN: No. But you should be supervised. And I shouldn't be with you any more. I shouldn't have been for at least a year, in fact.

MAGGIE: Well now you got what you wanted, didn't you.

QUENTIN: No, exactly the opposite. But he's trying to get a plane up here; if he can he'll spend the night with you; and you can decide with him what to do. But we shouldn't argue any more. It's between you and him.

MAGGIE, *with a knowing, determined smile*: You're not going to put *me* anywhere, mister.

QUENTIN: I've nothing to do with that, Maggie, it's you and him.

MAGGIE: Why, what'd you say to him?

QUENTIN: Maggie, you want to die and I don't know any more

how to prevent it. Maybe it was just my being out in the real world for twenty-four hours again, but it struck me that I'm playing with your life out of some idiotic hope of some kind that you're suddenly going to come out of this endless spell. I think somebody ought to be with you who has no illusions of that kind, and simply watches constantly to prevent it.

MAGGIE: Maybe a little love would prevent it.

QUENTIN: But how would you know, Maggie? Not that I love you, but if I did, would you know any more? Do you know who I am? Aside from my name? I'm all the evil in the world, aren't I? All the betrayal, the broken hopes, the murderous revenge?

MAGGIE: And how'd that happen? Takes two to tango, kid.

With a sneer she opens the bottle. He stands at once.

QUENTIN: I'm not sitting here if you take any more. Especially on top of whisky; that's the way it happened the last time.

She spills out a few into her palm and he walks a step away.

Okay. Carrie's in her room; I've told her to look in here every few minutes, and if she sees the signs she's to call the ambulance. Good night.

MAGGIE: She won't call the ambulance, she loves me.

QUENTIN: That's why she'll call the ambulance. Which is what I would have done last year if I'd loved you instead of loving myself. I'd have done it two years ago, in fact, but I didn't know what I know now.

MAGGIE, *sneering*: What do you know now? You're spoiled. What do you know?

QUENTIN: A suicide kills two people, Maggie. That's what it's for. So I'm removing myself and perhaps it will lose its point.

She appears to consider for a moment; then carefully takes two pills and swallows them.

Right.

He walks, determined, upstage. And when he is a far distance:

MAGGIE, *on a new level; softly, and without any antagonism*: What's Lazarus?

He halts, without turning back. She looks about for him, not knowing he has left.

Quentin?

Not seeing him, she starts up off the bed; a certain alarm . . .

Quen?

He comes halfway back.

QUENTIN: Jesus raised him from the dead. In the Bible. Go to sleep now.

MAGGIE: Wha's 'at suppose to prove?

QUENTIN: The power of faith.

MAGGIE: What about those who have no faith?

QUENTIN: They only have the will.

MAGGIE: But how you get the will?

QUENTIN: You have faith.

MAGGIE: Some apples.

He smiles, turns again to go.

I want more cream puffs.

He turns back; doesn't answer.

And my birthday dress? If I'm good? Mama? I want my mother.

She sits up, looks about as in a dream, turns and sees him.

Why you standing there?

She gets out of bed, squinting, and comes up to him, peers into his face; her expression comes alive.

You . . . you want music?

QUENTIN: All right, you lie down, and I'll put a little music on.

MAGGIE: No, you; you, sit down. And take off your shoes. I mean just to rest. You don't have to do anything. *She goes to the machine, turns it on; jazz.* Was I sleeping?

QUENTIN: For a moment, I think.

MAGGIE: Was she. . . . was anybody else here?

QUENTIN: No. Just me.

MAGGIE: Is there smoke?

QUENTIN: Your mother's dead and gone, dear, she can't hurt you any more, don't be afraid.

MAGGIE, *in a helpless voice of a child*: Where you going to put me?

QUENTIN, *his chest threatening a cry*: Nowhere, dear—he'll decide with you. He might be here tonight.

MAGGIE: See? I'll lay down. *She hurries to the bed, lies down.* See?

QUENTIN: Good.

MAGGIE: 'Member how used to talk to me till I went to sleep?

QUENTIN: Yes, dear. *He sits beside the bed.*

MAGGIE—*she struggles for lucidity, for some little pose of quiet charm*: It nice in Chicago?

QUENTIN: Yes, very nice. *The caricature of the pleasantry nearly shakes off the world.* Was it nice here?

MAGGIE—*she takes a strange, deep breath*: Ya. Some birds came. And a mouse. You . . . you could have the pills if you want.

QUENTIN—*stands*: I'll have Carrie come in and take them. *He starts to move.*

MAGGIE, *clutching the bottle*: No. I won't give them to Carrie.

QUENTIN: Why do you want me to have them?

MAGGIE, *extending them*: Here.

QUENTIN—*pause*: Do you see it, Maggie? Right now? You're trying to make me the one who does it to you? I take them; and then we fight, and then I give them up, and you take the death from me. You see what's happening? You've been setting me up for a murder. Do you see it? *He moves backward.* But now I'm going away; so you're not my victim any more. It's just you, and your hand.

MAGGIE, *slowly retracting her hand, looking at it*: But ask Ludwig— I only wanted to be wonderful so you be proud, and you—

QUENTIN: And for yourself, dear, mostly for yourself. You were ambitious; it's no crime. You would have been everything you are without me.

MAGGIE, *about to weep*: You ran out of patience, right?

QUENTIN: That's right. Yes.

MAGGIE: So you lied. Right?

QUENTIN: Yes, I lied. Every day. We are all separate people.

MAGGIE: You wanted a happy whore. Right?

QUENTIN: Not a whore, but happy, yes. I didn't want too much trouble.

MAGGIE: But Jesus must have loved her. Right?

QUENTIN: Who?

MAGGIE: Lazarus?

QUENTIN—*pause; he sees, he gropes toward his vision*: That's right, yes! He . . . loved her enough to raise her from the dead. But he's God, see . . .

> *Felice appears, raising her arm in blessing.*

. . . and God's power is love without limit. But when a man dares reach for that . . .

> *He has moved toward Felice, pursuing his truth.*

he is only reaching for the power. Whoever goes to save another person with the lie of limitless love throws a shadow on the face of God. And God is what happened, God is what is; and whoever stands between another person and her truth is not a lover, he is . . .

> *He breaks off, lost, peering, and turns back to Maggie for his clue, and as Felice vanishes . . .*

And then she said.

> *He goes back to Maggie, crying out to invoke her.*

And then she said!

MAGGIE—*she is trying to wipe a film from before her thought*: But . . . but . . . will my father find me if you put me. . . No. I mean . . . what's moral?

QUENTIN, *in the tension of trying to recall*: To tell the truth.

MAGGIE: No-no . . . against yourself even.

QUENTIN: Yes.

MAGGIE—*she turns to him; her look is insane, and the truth is purified of all restraint*: Well?

> *A cry is gathering in her, as though only now did she know there was no return.*

I hear you. Way inside. Quentin? My love? I hear you! Tell me what happened!

> *Her tears tell her sanity. He weeps facing her.*

QUENTIN, *on the verge of the abyss*: Maggie, we . . . used one another.

MAGGIE, *weeping, calling*: Not me, not me!

QUENTIN: Yes, you. And I. "To live," we cried, and "Now," we cried. And loved each other's innocence as though to love enough what was not there would cover up what was. But there is an angel, and night and day he brings back to us exactly what we want to lose. And no chemical can kill him, no blindness dark enough to make him lose his way; so you must love him, he keeps truth in the world. You eat those pills like power, but only what you've done will save you. If you could only say, I have been cruel, this frightening room would open! If you could say, I have been kicked around, but I have been just as inexcusably vicious to others; I have called my husband idiot in public, I have been utterly selfish despite my generosity, I have been hurt by a long line of men but I have cooperated with my persecutors. . . .

MAGGIE—*she has been writhing, furious at this exorcism*: Son of a bitch!

QUENTIN: And I am full of hatred, I, Maggie, the sweet lover of all life—I hate the world!

MAGGIE: Get out of here!

QUENTIN: Hate women, hate men, hate all who will not grovel at my feet proclaiming my limitless love for ever and ever!

> *She spills a handful of pills into her palm. He speaks desperately, trying not to physically take the pills from her.*

Throw them in the sea; throw death in the sea and drink your life instead; your rotten, betrayed, hateful mockery of a life. That power is death, Maggie! Do the hardest thing of all—see your own hatred, and live!

Dumbly, she raises her hand toward her open mouth. He cannot hold back his hand and grips her wrist.

MAGGIE: What are you, goddamn judge or something? Let go. You no judge.

He lets go.

You know when I wanted to die. When I read what you wrote, judgey. Two months after we were married, judgey.

QUENTIN, *stricken, afraid, but remorseless*: Let's keep it true. It's not some words on a piece of paper destroyed us. You told me you tried to die long before you met me.

MAGGIE: So you're not even there, huh. I didn't even meet you. *Tries to laugh.* You coward. Coward!

She staggers to her feet; he finds it hard to look directly at her. A clear line of accusation momentarily seems to steady her, and with the pills in her palm she stands straight.

I was married to a king, you son of a bitch! I was looking for a fountain pen to sign some autographs. And there's his desk . . .

She is speaking toward some invisible source of justice now, telling her injury.

. . . and there's his empty chair where he sits and thinks how to help people. And there's his handwriting. I wanted to touch his handwriting. And there's some words . . .

She almost literally reads in the air, and with the same original astonishment.

"The only one I will ever love is my daughter. If I could only find an honorable way to die."

Now she turns to him.

When you gonna face that, judgey? Remember how I fell down fainted? On the new rug? 'Member? That's what killed me, judgey. Right?

She staggers up to him and into his face.

'Zat right? When you gonna face that one, kiddo?

QUENTIN—*a pause; he is struggling with her accusation and his guilt*: All right. You pour them back and I'll tell you the truth about that.

MAGGIE: You won't tell truth.

QUENTIN: I will now. *He tries to tip her hand toward the bottle, holding both her wrists.* You can hold the bottle, just pour them back.

MAGGIE, *closing her hand on the pills*: But that's why, right?

QUENTIN, *with difficulty*: We'll see. Pour them back, first.

> *She lets him pour them back, but she keeps the bottle. She sits staring on the bed, holding it in two hands.*

MAGGIE—*she takes a deep breath*: Liar.

QUENTIN, *in quiet tension against his own self-condemnation*: We'd had our first party in our own house. Some important people, network heads, directors . . .

MAGGIE: And you were ashamed of me. Don't lie now! You're still playing God! That's what killed me, Quentin!

QUENTIN: All right. I wasn't . . . ashamed. But . . . afraid. *Pause.* I wasn't sure if any of them . . . had had you.

MAGGIE, *astounded*: But I didn't know any of those!

QUENTIN, *not looking at her*: I didn't know. But I swear to you, I did get to where none of it meant anything to me, I couldn't imagine what I'd ever been ashamed of. But it was too late. I had written that, and I was like all the others who'd betrayed you, and I could never be trusted again.

MAGGIE, *shaking her head; it is all corroborated*: You never gave me a chance!

QUENTIN, *consumed, desperate for the slightest absolution*: I did, Maggie, but it was too late. I laid down my life for you. But it was all too late.

MAGGIE, *with a mixture of accusation but near-sympathy*: Why did you write that? *She sobs, once.*

QUENTIN: Because when the guests had gone, and you suddenly turned on me, calling me cold, remote, it was the first time I saw your eyes that way—betrayed, screaming that I'd made you feel you didn't exist.

MAGGIE: Don't mix me up with Louise!

QUENTIN: That's just it. That I could have brought two women so different to the same accusation—it closed a circle for me. And I wanted to face the worst thing I could imagine—that I could not love. And I wrote it down, like a letter . . . from myself.

She pours pills into her hand again.

I've told you the truth. That's rock bottom. What more do you want?

She starts to raise her hand to her mouth, and he steps in and holds her wrist.

What more do you *want*?

She looks at him, her eyes unreadable.

Maggie, we've got to have some humility toward ourselves; we were both born of many errors, a human being has to forgive himself! You want me to say I killed you? All right, I killed you. Now what? What do you want?

A strange calm overtakes her. She lies back on the bed. The hostility seems to have gone.

MAGGIE: Just . . . be human. And help me. And stop arguing.

He lets her hand go; it falls to the bed.

And love me. Sit on the bed.

He sits down.

Cover me.

He covers her.

And take down the sand dune. It's not too expensive. I wanted to hear the ocean when we made love in here but we could never hear the ocean.

QUENTIN: We're nearly broke, Maggie; and that dune keeps the roof from blowing off.

MAGGIE: Then you get a new roof. You'll have them take it away, right?

He doesn't answer.

I'm cold. Lie on me.

QUENTIN: I can't do that again, not when you're like this.

MAGGIE: Please. Just till I sleep!

QUENTIN, *breaking down*: Maggie, it's a mockery. Leave me *something*.

MAGGIE: Just out of humanness! I'm cold!

> *Downing self-disgust, he lies down on her but holds his head away. Pause.*

If you don't argue with me any more, I'll get rid of that other lawyer. 'Kay? If you don't argue? Ludwig doesn't argue.

> *He is silent.*

And don't keep saying we're broke? And the sand dune?

> *The fear of his own total disintegration is growing in his face.*

'Cause I love the ocean sound; like a big mother—sssh, sssh, sssh.

> *He slips off and stands looking down at her. Her eyes are closed.*

You gonna be good now? 'Cause all I am . . . is love. And sex.

> *She takes a very deep, jagged breath.*

> *Quentin reaches in carefully and tries to slip the bottle out of her hand; she grips it.*

Whyn't you lie on me?

QUENTIN, *as a fact, simply*: It disgusts me.

MAGGIE: But if Lazarus . . .

QUENTIN: I am not the Savior and I am not the help. . . . You are not going to kill me, Maggie, and that's all this is for!

MAGGIE: You liar!

QUENTIN: Not any more—I am not guilty for your life! I can't be. But I am responsible for it now. And I want those pills. I don't want to fight you, Maggie. Now put them in my hand.

> *She looks at him; then quickly tries to swallow her handful, but he knocks some of them out—although she swallows many. He grabs for the bottle but she holds and he pulls, yanks; she goes with the force and he drags her onto the floor, trying to pry her hands open as she flails at him and tears at his face, digs at his eyes. Her strength is wild and no longer her own, and, strangely, she is smiling, almost laughing. He grabs her wrist and squeezes it with both his fists.*

Drop them, you bitch! You won't kill me!

She holds on, still smiling with a profound certainty, and suddenly, clearly, he lunges for her throat and lifts her with his grip.

You won't kill me! You won't kill me!

She drops the bottle as from the farthest distance Mother rushes to a point crying out—the toy sailboat in her hand—

MOTHER: Darling, open this door! I didn't trick you! I told Fanny to tell you we'd gone as soon you got up from your nap! I didn't trick you!

Quentin springs away from Maggie, who falls back to the floor; his hands are open and in air.

Quentin, why are you running water in there?

The sound of the sea comes up. Mother backs away in horror.

Stop that water! Quentin, I'll die if you do that! I saw a star when you were born, a light, a light in the world!

He stands transfixed as Mother backs into his hand, and he begins to squeeze her throat and she to sink to the floor gasping for breath. He releases her in horror.

QUENTIN: Murder?

Mother stumbles into darkness, her hands in prayer, whispering, "I will die, I will die." He turns to Maggie, who is now getting to her hands and knees, gasping. He rushes to help her, terrified by his realization, but she flails out at him, and on one elbow looks up at him in a caricature of laughter, her eyes victorious and wild with fear.

MAGGIE: Now we both know. You tried to kill me, mister. I been killed by a lot of people, some couldn't hardly spell, but it's the same, mister. You're on the end of a long, long line, Frank.

As though to ward off the accusation he desperately reaches again to help her up, and in absolute terror she skitters away across the floor.

Stay 'way! . . . No! No—no, Frank! Don't you do that!

Cautiously, as though facing a wild, ravening beast.

Don't you do that . . . or I call Quentin if you do that.

She glances off and calls quietly, but never leaving him out of her sight.

Quentin? Qu—?

She falls unconscious, crumpled on the floor, now with deep, strange breathing. He quickly goes to her, throws her over onto her stomach, starts artificial respiration, but just as he is about to start, he stands. He calls upstage.

QUENTIN: Carrie? Carrie!

Carrie appears, praying, with open hands almost shielding her eyes. And, as though it were a final farewell:

Quick! Call the ambulance.

Carrie bends to exorcise Maggie's demons.

Stop wasting time! Call the ambulance!

Carrie hurries out.

Felice appears; he hardly glances at her, comes down to the dock, halts. Felice remains behind him.

. . . No-no, we saved her. It was just in time. For her. But not for me. I knew why I had stayed; I packed up next morning. Her doctor tells me she had a few good months; he even thought for a while she was making it. Unless, God knows, he fell in love with her too.

He almost smiles; it is gone.

Look, I'll say it. It's really all I came to say. Barbiturates kill by suffocation. And the signal is a kind of sighing—the diaphragm is paralyzed.

With more difficulty.

And I'd noticed it when we'd begun to argue. . . . I know, it usually does subside, but if not—each second can be most precious, why waste them arguing? What can be so important to gamble her life to get?

The tower lights, fierce, implacable.

. . . My innocence, you see? To get that back you kill most easily. . . . No, don't; I want it . . . just the way it was.

He looks up.

And all those stars, still so fixed, so fortunate! And her precious seconds squirming in my hand like bugs; and I heard. Those deep, unnatural breaths, like the footfalls of my coming peace—and knew . . . I wanted them. How is that possible—I loved that girl!

> *Slight pause.*

And the name . . . yes, the name . . .

> *Louise appears, young, in her lab costume.*

. . . in whose name do you ever turn your back . . .

> *He looks out at the audience.*

. . . but in your own? In Quentin's name! Always in your own blood-covered name you turn your back!

> *Holga appears on the highest level.*

HOLGA: But no one is innocent they did not kill!

QUENTIN: But love, is love enough? What love, what wave of pity will ever reach this knowledge—I know how to kill. . . . I know, I know . . . she was doomed in any case, but will that cure? Or is it possible . . .

> *He turns toward the tower, moves toward it as toward a terrible God.*

. . . that this is not bizarre . . . to anyone? And I am not alone, and no man lives who would not rather be the sole survivor of this place than all its finest victims? What is the cure? Who can be innocent again on this mountain of skulls? I tell you what I know! My brothers died here . . .

> *He looks down at the fallen Maggie.*

. . . but my brothers built this place; our hearts have cut these stones! And what's the cure!

> *Father and Mother and Dan appear, and Lou and Mickey; all his people are in light now.*

. . . No, not love; I loved them all, all! And gave them willingly to failure and to death that I might live, as they gave me and gave each other, with a word, a look, a truth, a lie—and all in love!

HOLGA: Hello!

QUENTIN: But what will defend her?

He cries up to her.

That woman hopes!

She stands unperturbed, resolute.

Or is that . . .

Struck—to the Listener:

. . . exactly why she hopes, because she knows? What burning cities taught her and the death of love taught me—that we are very dangerous!

Staring, seeing his vision.

And that, that's why I wake each morning like a boy—even now, even now! I swear to you, there's something in me that could dare to love this world again! . . . Is the knowing all? To know, and even happily that we meet unblessed; not in some garden of wax fruit and painted trees, that lie of Eden, but after, after the Fall, after many, many deaths. Is the knowing all? And the wish to kill is never killed, but with some gift of courage one may look into its face when it appears, and with a stroke of love—as to an idiot in the house—forgive it; again and again . . . forever?

He is evidently interrupted by the Listener, glances at his watch.

. . . Yes, I don't want to be late. Thanks for making time for me. . . . No, it's not certainty, I don't feel that. But it does seem feasible . . . not to be afraid. Perhaps it's all one has. I'll tell her that. . . . Yes, she will, she'll know what I mean. Well, see you again some time. Good luck, and thanks.

He turns upstage. He hesitates; all his people face him. He walks past Louise, pausing; but she turns her face away. He goes on and pauses beside Mother, who lowers her head in uncomprehended sorrow, and gestures as though he touched her chin and she looks up at him and dares a smile, and he smiles back. He pauses at his dejected Father and Dan, and with a look he magically makes them stand. Felice is about to raise her hand in blessing—he shakes her hand, aborting her enslavement. Mickey and Lou are standing together; he looks at them and neither of them are looking at him, but they move in behind him. Now he arrives at Maggie; she rises from the floor webbed in with demons, trying to awake. And with his life following him he climbs toward Holga, who raises her arm as though seeing him, and speaks with great love.

HOLGA: Hello!

He comes to a halt a few yards from her. A whispering goes up from all his people. He straightens against it and walks toward her, holding out his hand.

QUENTIN: Hello.

The darkness takes them all.

The play was directed by Elia Kazan and produced by Robert Whitehead for the Lincoln Center Repertory Company. It was first performed on January 23, 1964, at the ANTA–Washington Square Theatre, New York City.

THE CAST

(In order of appearance)

QUENTIN	Jason Robards, Jr.
FELICE	Zohra Lampert
HOLGA	Salome Jens
DAN	Michael Strong
FATHER	Paul Mann
MOTHER	Virginia Kaye
NURSES	Faye Dunaway, Diane Shalet
MAGGIE	Barbara Loden
ELSIE	Patricia Roe
LOU	David J. Stewart
LOUISE	Mariclare Costello
MICKEY	Ralph Meeker
MAN IN PARK	Stanley Beck
CARRIE	Ruth Attaway
LUCAS	Harold Scott
CHAIRMAN	David Wayne
HARLEY BARNES	Hal Holbrook
PORTER	Jack Waltzer
MAGGIE'S SECRETARY	Crystal Field
PIANIST	Scott Cunningham
OTHERS	Clint Kimbrough, John Phillip Law, Barry Primus, James Greene